WARNING:
THE FULL SERIES CONTAINS BEAUTIFUL PEOPLE
DOING BAD THINGS AND PACKS INTENSE SCENES
RANGING FROM TRAUMATIC TO SPICY AS THE
ACTION AMPLIFIES AND THE PLOT INTENSIFIES.
THIS SERIES IS NOT AN EROTIC SERIES, HOWEVER
THERE ARE ORGANIC LOVE SCENES, A FEW BEING
GRAPHIC IN NATURE. MATURE AUDIENCES ONLY.
NOT INTENDED FOR UNDERAGED READERS.

SIDE EFFECTS MAY INCLUDE BUT AREN'T LIMITED
TO:

- GRIPING AT PROTAGONIST'S STUPID CHOICES
- QUESTIONING YOUR OWN MORALITY
- TWISTS AND TURNS YOU DON'T SEE COMING
- MISSING TIME WITH LOVED ONES
- LOST SLEEP
- RAPID PAGE TURNING

NIGHTSHADE SERIES FACTS

PORTION SIZE	1 Novel after another

AMOUNT PER VOLUME 1

DON'T CLOSE YOUR EYES

Crime	**30%**
Suspense	45%
Mystery	50%
Thriller	10%
Romance	**70%**
Forced Proximity	4%
Love Triangle	80%
I Know He's Bad for Me, But…	90%
Drama	**58%**
Morally Gray Musing	60%

*The % Daily Value (DV) tells you the entertainment levels in the introductory volume of the Nightshade Series and contributes to an overall ability to escape reality.

This is a genre-blended series. Every volume is a mixture of suspense, crime, mystery, and romance, including elements of thriller and action/adventure, but each volume contains different levels of these ingredients.

CAST OF CHARACTERS

- **Klive Henley King** – mysterious anti-hero, anti-villain; Complicated Moonlight; Kinsley's pirate; lives double life
- **Kinsley Fallon Hayes** – Protagonist, bartender, college student in graduate school, Renowned sprinter dubbed Micro Machine
- **Jase Taylor** – Navy SEAL, bar singer, lifeguard
- **Rustin Keane** – Jase's childhood best friend
- **Nightshade** – Crime Syndicate
- **Inferno** – motorcycle club comprised of firefighters
- **Joey** – Klive's Personal Protective Detail (bodyguard)
- **Tyndall Taylor** – Jase's little sister, Kinsley's best friend
- **Andrew** (Andy) and **Clairice** (Claire) **Hayes** – Kinsley's parents
- **Bayleigh & Garrett** - Kinsley's co-workers
- **Marcus** – Kinsley's boss at the bar
- **Jarrell & Gustav** – lead bouncers at the bar
- **Rock–N–Awe** – Jase's band
- **Constance** – co-lead singer with Jase, Kinsley's friend
- **Ian Walton** – Kinsley's personal trainer and track coach
- **Lucy** (Looney Lucy), **Lindsay, Eliza, Julie** – track teammates
- **Sara Scott** – Kinsley's co-worker, Patrick Scott's wife
- **Patrick Scott** – Inferno prospect, Sara Scott's husband
- **Adrian Miller** – Kinsley's elective art professor

Don't close your
eyes, stay up reading
instead!

For AJ, the Lieutenant Commander who taught me to take control of my life and crap from no one.

&

For you, dear reader. Typing made me a writer. Publishing made me an author. You make sharing worth the effort.

CHAPTER 1

KLIVE

Murder was never my intended occupation.

"Please! I don't have your gold!" He darted a frantic look over his shoulder and rushed away from the festivities.

"Liar!" I stalked after him like an immortal serial killer. "I saw you onboard *The Banana Hamick* in the flotilla! You stood right next to the scalawag who stole *my* treasure! The chest was open at your feet! Where is it?!"

My hand rested on the handle of the long sword holstered in a scabbard at my waist. I debated whether to use the period piece or pull my modern pistol. A pirate would've used a sword, but the blood would cast off and make a mess. Shots kept the scene clean.

He tossed a handful of doubloons and a string of plastic pearls like he still marched in the parade. "This is all I have!" A miniature rubber duck fell from his pocket and squeaked under my boot seconds later. Gone was the smiling pirate who'd floated in beside the *Jose Gasparilla* and helped secure the key to the City of Tampa. Now, having cornered himself between a building and the choppy waters of the bay biting the bulkhead, he turned into a coward. His shaky finger pointed at the ground. "I promise. That's all. *That's* the gold that was on our boat. It's not real. They're replicas."

I paused my pursuit and dug the toe of my boot against the coin, watched the trinket disintegrate into white powder *worth* its weight in gold. "Exactly, mate."

The black makeup around his eyes ran in sweaty rivulets down his beaded cheeks. He shook his head, his hat wobbling. "I don't understand."

"Oh, I think you do," I said with a cruel smile. "Did your boss give this as a free sample? A treat for your being a good little minion? Where did he put the rest?"

"I promise, I don't know!" He sobbed when another pirate stepped around me. Four more fell in around us. He twisted, eyes darted every direction, devoid of solutions. His neck tensed while he swallowed, lips quivered as he raised his hands like he was under arrest. "I swear! I—"

"Enough!" I shouted.

His knees buckled before he fell, hands splayed on the concrete. Almost every digit decorated with costume jewelry.

My heavy foot falls stopped shy of grinding his fingers into the ground. I squatted and displayed my left hand beneath his eyes. "See this ring?"

"Mmhmm." A tear splashed the toe of my boot while his hat toppled from his head.

One of my Krewe kicked him in the stomach. "What'd you say, you disrespectful sonuva—"

My palm silenced him while the man wretched like he may vomit. I gripped his sweat-soaked hair and commanded him to meet my eyes. He blinked rapid tears until they trailed down his face. "Please. Please, don't kill me. I didn't know what they were. I thought they were fake—"

"Where. *Are.* They?!"

"Last I saw, they're still on the boat. Mick told us to grab the beads and leave the treasure, that it was too heavy to carry."

My chin jerked to three of my men. One lifted a phone and told the others to board the cigarette boat bobbing in the bay. I kept my grip on the man's hair and lifted him to his feet as I stood to my full height and looked down on him.

"Please—"

"Silence." I released his hair and stepped back, pulled my sword. His knees turned to jelly again. One of my remaining Krewe caught him under the arms. "Here's what's going to happen, mate. You have two choices. Walk the plank, or lose your head."

He balked as his chin snapped toward the white caps slamming the bulkhead. His lips formed voiceless words like silent prayers. He nodded, and I allowed my man to release him. We watched him turn toward the violent churning and march like a man determined to die with dignity.

"Oh, and before you go," I called, "if you live through this and we learn you lied, Nightshade's coming for you, and it won't be my men. *I'll* take personal pleasure in hunting you myself. Clear?"

His chin trembled once more before he stammered, "Ye-ye-yes, s-sir."

Like a man who'd lose his nerve if he lingered a second longer, he got a running start and his limbs flailed as he jumped over the edge and landed in the water. We watched as several pirate-themed rubber ducks floated to the surface and carried out with the current.

I sheathed my sword and toed the discarded beads, found another coin.

"Think he's drowning?" Eric asked me.

"Unless he strips out of his costume under there, yeah." I passed him the coin, watched him inspect the detailing.

He twisted and turned the shiny sheen in the twilight, nodded his approval. "They're exquisitely done. Beautiful work, Boss."

"Thanks, mate. I need you to join Nightshade and take the treasure to the locker for distribution. Make it look like you're actors cleaning up your boss's boat after the parade."

"And *The Banana Hamick*?" Eric and I rolled our eyes at 'Mick's' play on words with the bright yellow cigarette boat. "Want us to weigh anchor and let her float out to sea, make the captain go down with the ship?"

"Hell no. We'll take *The Banana Hamick* on a victory voyage to show Mick what it feels like when someone steals *his* treasure. Then maybe we'll toss him overboard and paint it black. Keep it for Nightshade."

"Now, that's a fun idea."

As I watched Eric place the cocaine doubloon on the planks beside the water's rising edge, I dug into my pocket for a fist-full of purple petals, then laid them in a row where they'd catch the lip of the wood rather than billow away in the breeze.

Atropa belladonna, also known as Deadly Nightshade—a poisonous plant producing edible fruit featured in *Macbeth* to stupefy an army before slaughter. The physical property of Satan himself, psychoactive or medicinal depending upon the hands wielding the power of the tiny flower—these I mixed with violet rose petals.

As we searched the white caps for signs of the pirate's body, I pondered whether Eve had eaten from a nightshade species in the Garden of Eden. Through Nightshade the knowledge of good and evil traversed hands to mouths, pricked between toes and fingers, inside forearms, snorted up noses, dipped inside body cavities depending upon a user's drug of choice. No longer was cocaine a thing of the past, but making a comeback. While others killed their customers with fentanyl, we preferred repeat clientele.

Eric and I blended into the crowded chaos of the Gasparilla festival-goers. The family-friendly daylight faded into merry mischief. A man in a kick-ass costume took the stage and sang the beginning of *Renegade* by Styx. The audience joined like a choir, then burst to life when the instruments decimated the last remaining calm.

Eric tipped his hat and headed in the direction of the flotilla. I mounted an elevated platform and smirked to myself as I looked over my proverbial kingdom. The wealthy elites bought and paid their way onto those parade floats they'd waved from earlier in the afternoon. I was one of them, but I was also one of few with true power, as were my hunters. We preyed under the shade of night, hence Nightshade.

Boisterous laughing accompanied clinking goblets and drunken jokes.

Within shadows of their play, we performed tricks in their distraction much the way puppeteers cast terrifying images across a backlit sheet from clean hands. Nightshade were masters of illusion, confusion, manipulation, and chaotic creation, all while blending into and within our environment. Magicians with manslaughter on our minds.

Ways to slaughter the prick from *The Banana Hamick* went into overdrive when Eric said through the bluetooth in my ear, "Mick's in the wind. He left in a hurry and took the gold. One bag fell from the chest. A trail of coins led us to the parade route."

I cursed. "That means he hopped a float, the little prat." I trotted down the platform and stalked toward the exit. "He fucked with the wrong kingpin. I'm going to the office to get out of this bloody costume, then going hunting. Meet me at the locker in an hour."

"Aye, aye, Captain."

"That's what I like to hear."

CHAPTER 2
KLIVE

The cacophony faded to white noise as I walked to the high-rise. I entered the car park and took the stairwell up to the second floor, then entered the building and called for the lift. A janitor paused vacuuming.

"Damn!" Sam gushed. "Best costume I've seen all day. I almost didn't recognize you with eyeliner, Mr. King."

"Thanks." I chuckled, pleased I now had a witness with a timestamp.

"Is that a *real* sword?"

The lift arrived with a ping. "Ask me no questions." The doors split, and I stepped aboard. "I'll tell you no lies." I tapped my smile. "Have a good night, mate!"

"You too!" he called just as the doors closed. I pressed for the twenty-seventh floor, leaned against the wall, and fished the Bowie knife from my coat. The tip of the blade dug gingerly beneath one of my fingernails, removing what I surmised to be my vic's makeup-stained sweat.

The elevator halted on the twenty-second floor.

What the—who the bloody hell is working on—? My

thoughts died as the doors divided. My stare landed on round hips wrapped in leather pants, corset, cleavage adorned with a bow, slender throat, lacy choker, parted lips. *Damn.*

The knife fell to my side while my mouth dried and fell open.

"Whoa!" She backed away. Beautiful green eyes, clouded with smeared mascara, widened. "I didn't expect anyone else." She shook her head, top hat firmly in place. "I'll catch the next one."

"I don't mind sharing," I said, a mite breathless, and forced a swallow.

"That's okay," she insisted too forcefully. "I'd rather be alone. Thank you."

My brows drew together. *Why call for the lift, then? How would it stop unless she'd pressed to go upstairs? Was she headed to the atrium?*

The doors closed, but I shoved the blade between them, sliced them apart.

"Oh, no!" Her palm shot out while she backed away. "No! No, thank you! You go!"

"Wait." I took in my knife, then ripped the blade flat against my chest. "It's not what it looks like."

"You leave, or I'll call the cops!"

"No, love, I didn't mean to use the bloody knife to open the lift! Gah! I mean *elevator!*"

High-heeled boots dashed behind the vacant reception desk. "I mean it!" she yelled. Fingers fumbled with the phone until the receiver clattered off the edge. "Oh, shit!" She sprinted down the hallway, tested office doors like a bimbo in a B-movie, a cell phone in her free hand.

"Look, I'm leaving!" I pressed for the parking garage rather than my office upstairs. "You have *nothing* to fear!" I sheathed the knife. *Pathetic girl. I ought to show her how to escape a killer rather than cornering herself!*

The doors closed, and I descended. Maybe I could change into something Nightshade had in the storage locker?

Why was her makeup messed up? Was someone with her? The more I thought about her odd behavior, the phone in her hand, her choosing the reception phone instead, the more her panic spelled the sort after trauma. *Recent* trauma. *Was she attacked? Did they attack her* here? *Was she running right back into danger?*

I hit the button for the next floor on the countdown. Exiting the elevator, I jogged back upstairs into the reception area, padded across the lobby, and re-cradled the screeching phone receiver. I saw no sign of her. *Had she fled into the other lift?* I looked up at the floor indicators. The one I'd departed continued down the floors to the parking garage. The other sat idle on the twelfth floor.

In the silence, a woman's voice drifted as a distant echo. *The lavatory!*

My six, nine, and twelve were clear, but I pulled my knife from inside my coat again and inched along the hallway of locked office doors. Darkness showed beneath sets of closed vertical blinds. I studied each for movement beyond, shoes beneath, reached for the sixth sense of lurking eyes. Every whispered step closer to her grieved voice amplified my adrenaline. I refused to heed the voice of reason shouting at me to flee as if *I* were prey. No attacker jumped to face me. No one scurried to escape from any of the offices I passed. No one in the lobby called for the lift. The atmosphere radiated the presence of the two of us alone.

"—ugh. Why won't anyone answer? Please ..."

My ear pressed against the door of the ladies' room.

Overhead, a florescent light twitched. The buzz mixed with the young woman's voice leaching through the wood.

"Daddy, something—" She strangled a sob. "—*awful* happened at the festival!" *Sob.* "Did Nate tell you what he did?" *Hoarse cry.* "He—I can't anymore." *Throat clearing. Sniffling. Stronger tone.* "I'm okay. My phone is dying. If you can't reach me, don't freak. I might stop at Constance's place tonight. Wanted you to know. Love you."

The beep of disconnection echoed off the tile walls. Unable to see her, I assumed the smack afterward was her phone against the granite countertop.

"Stupid, Kinsley! Stupid! Stupid! *Stupid!*" she shouted. I cursed under my breath and pulled away to spare my eardrum before braving the door again.

Silence. Sniffles.

Kinsley ....

I pressed harder to hear her, hoped she wouldn't scream again. She released a heavy exhale. "Okay, Kins. Don't be a coward. Call the cops. Let them deal with those creeps and that psycho with the knife, then go home. No one will know it was you. Totally anonymous."

Cops?

Wait—was I the psycho *with the knife? I hadn't done anything!*

I clutched the door handle.

She blew her nose, sniffled again. Before I did something daft, like walk in on her and demand an explanation, I lost my give-a-damn and strode to the lift. *She was fine. This floor was empty. All drama and foolishness. Let her report a pirate in a building! The police had* thousands *to sort through tonight.*

I paused before the door to the stairwell, but why take the stairs if I had nothing to hide? I'd committed no crime...*here.* My thumb pounded the call button, then I pulled my pocket watch and cursed the lift's sluggish climb back upstairs, the time I'd wasted worrying over the little wench, the change in my plans. At the sound of her gasp, the halves of my watch snapped shut in my fist, heart lurched to my throat.

"You said you were leaving," she said.

"And *you said* I was a psycho with a knife. Therefore, we are both liars." The lift arrived with a ping. I kept my back to her as I boarded, then braved her beauty with a scowl on my face to conceal my inexplicable nerves and prior awe. "I came to check on you, however, I now find it best to leave you to your pity party."

Her cheeks blossomed with embarrassment. The apprehension in her frame sagged with shame. Her skin wasn't a mess anymore, but her nose was pink. Somehow the color amplified the emerald tones in her bright irises, so beguiling, bewitching, bewildering ....

I fought a wave of guilt when a fresh sheen of unshed tears glossed her glances anywhere else. She wasn't one of my men, a subordinate, a criminal, a target, or, well, anyone.

Exactly.

Her gaze darted to my face. "You followed me?"

Dumb question. "I've wasted enough time. I'm leaving. Good night." *And good riddance.* I stabbed the 'door close' button.

Just before the doors sealed, the girl rushed inside.

Bloody hell! I jolted against the side wall.

She reached for the panel of numbers. I threw my arm to block her.

She ripped back. "What the hell?"

"Your makeup was a mess before I startled you."

"What?"

"Your eyes." I gestured with one hand, pocketed the other. "You fixed them, but black tears covered your face. *Before* I found you in your fit. Wasn't me you needed to call the cops on. What happened tonight?"

She stared, her only movement a swallow and an artery jumping in her lace-adorned throat. Her breathing ceased. Red splotches painted her chest and neck.

"Please answer the question."

Her cleavage fell with a harsh exhale. "It's none of your business. Why are you carrying a knife like *that* in a place like *this*?"

My head angled. *Was that all she could think of? My knife?*

"Perhaps this *should* be the business of the one with the knife." My hand rested on my costume, over the knife tucked in my pocket again. "You see, love, in case you couldn't tell, I also attended Gasparilla and planned to protect myself while I was there."

"You use Mace to protect yourself at Gasparilla, not a machete." Her nervous eyes jumped to my sheathed sword.

The space filled with my unexpected laughter. "Pepper spray? Is that what you used to fend off the bloke who left the fingerprints on your arm?"

She gasped and slapped her palm over the exact spot. A pink glow expanded up her temples.

"Who hurt you?" My jaw clenched and lifted while I stood straight to look down on her, like I could intimidate her into giving me the info.

Her gaze collected worry as she studied our confines like a cornered creature.

"It's not like that." *Great; the type to protect an abuser.*

"Then what *is* it like?" I all but growled. The thief in the *Banana Hamick* may not be tonight's only target.

"I don't wanna talk about it. I don't even know you." She reached around me for the button. I shifted between her and the column altogether. "Ugh! Come on!"

"Hey. If someone did something, I'd rather take care of it than not. You're safe with me, but don't protect some asshole."

With sudden courage, she narrowed her eyes with a mute implication that *I* was the asshole for the moment.

"*Nothing* happened. Not in the manner you're thinking."

"Right." I clenched my jaw and held firm. "We're not moving until you elaborate."

She drilled a scowl through my skull. I allowed silence to expand the interrogation. She caved in less than ten seconds. "Fine," she sighed the word with an added 'uh' tacked to the end. "My boyfriend stood me up. I put on this stupid costume because he loves Gasparilla. We were s'posed to meet at three this afternoon. I waited till dark, then admitted defeat."

"Did you call him to make sure—"

"He's ghosting me. He saw my texts. Like I said, he stood me up."

Who'd be so foolish? Whatever was the matter with him? Or, maybe she was a pill? Pretty, but poisonous...? What if he were actually the one fleeing for his poor life?

"How did you end up here?" I asked, willing myself to be correct so I might leave without guilt.

"Gah," she growled. "You want my life story, too? My father works here. I was hoping he was still in the office. So, you see, I was running to Daddy because my boyfriend hurt my *wittle* feelings. Happy now? Should I apologize for wounding your arrogant pride?"

Poisonous, indeed. On an aggravated whistle, I hammered the button for the car park, then balled my sweaty hands inside the deep pockets of my pirate coat. If she were going to a different floor, she could press her own button for grating against mine.

"I'm sorry." She suddenly deflated.

"So, pout about it. Seems your solution of choice."

Her jaw dropped like she was ready to ream my ass. "How *dare* you! *You* asked! I told you I didn't want to talk about it." She peeked at the red indicator, then pressed the next floor. "I don't need your trash." Seconds later, she jumped off like I was diseased. The doors closed, and I let them. I didn't need her garbage either.

What did that little wench matter?

I shattered the seconds of silence with a slew of curses and stabbed a button three floors further down.

The moment the doors cracked, I darted into the stairwell. Who the hell knew why.

Racing heels clacked down the stairs. The corridor echoed with her choked sobs. *Was she crying over* him *or* my *unleashing on the wrong target? What was wrong with me?*

I let the heavy door slam. She cursed. I heard her turn and jog back upstairs. This girl's survival instincts wouldn't stand a chance against a true predator. *Perhaps what led her to whomever left those bruises on her arm?* Rage unfurled at the idea, her bloke leaving her to the mercy of someone after she'd dressed provocatively for him.

"Come on! It's only me!" I shouted up through the space where the railing wound around each level. The clattering paused. She leaned over from two floors above.

"Oh, and that's supposed to make me feel better?" she shouted. "Leave me alone!"

"Yeah? And leave you at the mercy of a pervert lurking in dark places like these?" I clapped back.

"You mean like *you*?" she fired.

"I mean like the wanker you're covering for! *Blast!*" I leapt away as she spit. Her saliva missed me and continued down the fifteen remaining flights. A moment later, a steel door slammed. No more footsteps.

Hell no! Now it was personal.

CHAPTER 3
KLIVE

I ripped the exit open and stormed to the elevator, mashed the button. The floor indicator ticked down. Once the doors split, I half-expected her not to be inside, but there she stood, hands curled around the bar against the back wall. Her glare blazed with anger, but beneath it flashed something challenging. Mine mirrored the sentiment.

"I didn't deserve that." I gave her my back while I pressed for the garage once more. "Any of it."

"The hell you didn't," she stammered. "You shouldn't have left the elevator, I told you to leave me alone, and I'm not covering for anyone. You were chasing me, for goodness' sake!"

My eyes flared, and I turned with incredulous disbelief at her foolish bravery. "*Chasing* you? Shame on me for trying to be chivalrous."

"*Chivalrous?*" She scoffed. "You call that chivalry when you practically wore the inconvenience of all this upstairs? I wasn't planning on you interrupting me either, bud."

I shook my head, unable to help my disgust. "No wonder your bloke stood you up."

She flinched like I'd slapped her. The heaving in her chest returned. Lunging forward, she halted our progress, then twisted to face me. Her bravado soon wavered under my silent scrutiny.

"Young lady, I haven't time to play your childish games." I reached toward the panel. She jolted back against the column of buttons before melting down on the marble beneath our feet. Multiple floors lit, but that didn't strike me as much as her presumption that I'd strike her.

"You're right." Her voice cracked as her face fell into her hands. "I deserved it. I'm a terrible girlfriend."

I hadn't an umbrella adequate enough for her infantile rain of emotion. With a sigh, I knelt and cupped my hands beneath her arms to lift her to her feet, bracing for the spit likely to splat in my eye.

"Forgive me if I scared you again, love, but why not spit in his face instead of mine?"

"Why do you assume I won't?" she asked in bitterness.

We stopped on the first of twelve additional levels. She stared at me, I stared at her, until the doors closed once more. Interesting. She'd just conceded a perfect moment to escape. With eleven bloody floors to go, I prodded her places of pain.

"Let's pretend I believe you. Why meltdown over this bloke? How much time have you wasted on him?"

"In light of tonight, too much." She looked everywhere but at me. Her eyes ran out of space and traveled up to mine, big, beseeching, apologetic. "I'm sorry I've wasted yours."

That look loaded the bullet in a mental game of Russian roulette.

Drop the pistol and leave the risk!

Fresh tears added to her a different vulnerability that unsettled my normal control. Even if I knew she was lying, I'd been an insensitive asshole. *Fix it. But how?*

The doors opened again. *No way was I doing this ten more times.* I herded her from our cell to press the button for the other one. She argued the whole way out, bargaining for using the extra floors for contemplation.

"You mean for wallowing? There's nothing to contemplate. If something is finished, let it be, and move on," I commanded. The indicator counted up from the parking level. The bell chimed. The doors split open, but she didn't budge.

"I'll wait for the next one, thanks," she said.

Pft! No way in hell I'd concede with the visual and emotional target she'd painted on herself. Add the foolish fight-or-flight responses, she was prime for the wrong prick. *Not on my watch.*

"Nonsense. Come now." Plying her was like taking a stubborn jackass for a walk. After another verbal battle with her attitude, the bloody doors that kept trying to pinch us, my patience snapped. I spun her and cinched her waist in my grip.

"Oh!" She gasped while she grabbed my shoulders. I somewhat lost my head as the ribbons crisscrossing the length of her spine danced like feathers in a bow over my fingertips. Her body shifted closer. Whether I'd tugged her, or she'd leaned in, I couldn't say. I only knew I wasn't getting enough oxygen as her chest brushed mine, the pretty bow begging to be untied for the gift inside.

Her fingers laced together at the nape of my neck. My lips parted on a long, steady breath. Her eyelids fell a fraction as she watched. When I stroked my thumbs against her waist, she bit her lower lip as I felt a tremor travel through her like she was sensitive to my touch. Tension compounded as the doors sealed us inside the private cocoon.

My tone firm yet gentle, I powered through.

"Look at me, love." Look at me, she did. Up close, her irises heated like the blood pounding my veins. My gaze strayed to her gnawed lip for relief.

I hardened my expression and resolve while I warred with fantasies of pressing her against the wall to taste the cinnamon of her breath.

"Enough of this," I said almost to myself. "Don't waste your time drafting excuses for someone else's misbehavior. Quit looking for your father to coddle you. For the sake of your self-esteem, stop dating little boys. They've no fortitude." My mind clouded with dangerous inspiration while she searched my face. Angry tears glazed her eyes like puddles of gasoline. My desire sparked like a pyromaniac holding a Zippo lighter. One strike may cause a beautiful explosion.

No woman had ever looked at me like I had the power to put away her pain, even though I'd had a hand in causing hers. *Why did she?*

"I swear," I whispered aloud what ought to remain in my mind, "you would be so strong with a real man." *With me*, I finished with my eyes.

She gasped, conflicted and offended. Her brows dipped while she read my eyes like she understood the words written in my mind. I sensed the same about reading hers. *This* young woman didn't need a kid causing drama. She needed the adrenaline rush of being shoved to the precipice of a cliff, then yanked back to safety by someone who couldn't resist her before he brought her to combustion.

"Come to Gasparilla with me," I blurted, mutinous against tonight's priorities, my bad side, those who controlled me.

"No." She released a shaky breath.

Curse that word again!

She broke my grasp to push the garage button I'd neglected.

"I don't date strangers," she said like she'd hardened her own resolve.

"Perhaps you should."

She arched her eyebrow. "Nope."

"Coffee then?" I asked. "To get to know one another?" The floors ticked down like a time bomb closer to detonating and obliterating every conflicted second with her!

"The coffee shop is closed on Saturdays."

"I know. We don't have to go to this shop or the festival. We can go anywhere you want." I shifted to close the small distance between us, desperate to be near her once more, but she shook her head.

"I think you've gotten the wrong impression of me."

"Ditto."

She scrunched her nose. "No, I mean this." She added space between us and gestured to her attire. "This isn't me. For starters, I don't dress like a ho, I'm not easy, and dating isn't that simple. I don't need a consolation prize. I need to get away from *you*."

Ouch! How could she say that when she'd been wanton in my grasp moments ago?

The lift opened on the parking garage. Humidity glued to our skin, as thick and uncomfortable as the chemistry between us. We surveyed the dimly lit expanse. Few cars remained. She was lucky I was here, though my pride ached to hell.

"Great," I said. "I'm too complicated to give you consolation, nor do I date. I was merely softening the bruise to your abandoned ego." I propped one hand against the door. My other gestured she exit first. Under normal circumstances, I'd have relished wounding someone who'd wounded me, but I loathed the flush of pain in her expression. No different from what she'd done to me, but this stung.

"Anyone ever tell you what an asshole you are?" High heels hammered the concrete as she left.

I swallowed. "All the time, love."

"I hate this. I'm done with men and their drama. It's all the same. And *you're*...." She trailed off in search of a word that might match how low I measured, inspecting me for flaws. Rosy blossoms on the apples of her cheeks betrayed her. *That's right, love, I'm not alone in this inexplicable attraction and misery.*

"I'm what?" I taunted. "Grown up? Mature? Too big a prick?" Better if she hated me to escape my attention. Safer for both of us.

"Too *old*?" The corners of her lips lifted like that mental Russian roulette revolver. Her expressive eyes spun the cylinder as I stared like a victim realizing too late his own number was up. Victorious knowing fired from her irises, nailing my contempt, bleeding my strength. She turned and stalked away, determined to hold the power over me tight in her little fist.

Not so fast.

"You're not done. If you'd had a man instead of a boy, you'd be done with drama, because real men don't have time for theatrics. Nor do real men hurt women. You're finished with temperamental kids. Maybe ring me when you're not one anymore." I strolled behind her, enjoying the line of her legs in Puss-in-Boots stilettos.

"What are you doing?" She spun so fast I stumbled into her. Her squeal echoed off the concrete pillars while I grabbed her to keep us both from falling. Warm hands wrapped around my neck. Fiery eyes blazed mine with accusation. *Uh, huh. Two can play this game.*

"Did you do that on purpose?" I grinned.

"Ha! You wish." She stabilized and threw a finger in my face. The weak girl vaporized to re-materialize into a dominating woman. Pure beauty. This young lady, *Kinsley*, was *the* Anne Bonny to my Calico Jack...*Kinsley King has quite the ring ....*

"I asked you a question." She interrupted my reverie. "What are you doing?"

I blinked hard. *What was I doing? Hell, what was I thinking?*

"Dangerous to be alone in a parking garage at night dressed so sexy." I nodded toward her costume. "Here. Take this." I shrugged out of my pirate coat.

"Oh, the chivalry angle again?" She stared at my offering with a stubborn lift of her chin. When I raised my eyebrows, she grimaced and yanked the heavy crushed velvet from my hand. She shrugged into the sleeves much longer than her arms. Anne Bonny looked mighty adorable in my coat. Too adorable to sport such a venomous attitude.

"Lead the way," I told her.

She snorted. "I don't think so."

My finger rose this time. "I'm walking you to your car."

"Why? To put me in my car seat and buckle my belt?"

"If you need it, sure, but I figured you'd at least graduated to a booster seat." She was so frustrated I barely contained a grin. "In those heels, I bet you can even reach the pedals."

"Insults coming from Peter Pan in a Captain Hook costume? That's cute."

I winced like she'd burned me before my wicked smile spread. "Oh, come now, love. At least grant me a solid Captain Morgan."

"Yeah, I could use a few shots of rum after being around you."

I chuckled. She turned to keep kwalking. Her pace quickened. I kept up, and she grumbled as we narrowed in on a shiny green Civic. The unmistakable feeling of watching eyes skittered over my back, raising goosebumps on my neck. Glancing around like she sensed danger, too, she pulled the coat closed. Her eyes held mine for a ghost of a second. We were being observed. She rushed to her car with new urgency while I scanned for threats. *God help Mick if he thought to war with me here.*

She had my knife. I'd rather not pull my pistol or the sword unless I had to.

Improvisations formulated as she unlocked her car, the lights flashing once. I reached for her door, but she spun with a scolding index pointing at my face again. A great effort with the sleeve.

"No," she said. "You don't get to open my door. Funny how you don't have time for childish games, yet you're the one playing them."

"Am not—"

"Are, too. Know what I'm done with? Fear. Everyone knows boys have a fear of commitment. I shouldn't be heartbroken about being stood up. It's always *coming* as long as they're not allowed to. And here I have a man—" She poked my chest. "—arguing like a child while lecturing me like I'm the weak one, when he'd likely walk away for the same reasons? It takes real strength to hold out for what you want, so admit it. Which of us is weakest? Who's the kid? Be honest."

"W-*whoa!*" I stammered, amusement confiscated. Hers was, too.

What had this bloke done to her? Dumped her over sex? Forced her without permission after she'd changed her mind?

Her finger stayed in place. I wrapped my hand around her fist and leaned in to convey the severity in my gaze. "You're *wrong.*"

She snorted and speared my eyes with a dare to prove otherwise. "You're weak. You're afraid. You're all the same."

Anne Bonny shoved me aside to open the car door by herself and plunked into the driver's seat. I grabbed the door before she closed me out. My bravado challenged, she was testing me, but I was too angry at my imagination and her comparing me to that boy.

"No," I measured, "I'm not. It's complicated. *I'm complicated.* I will say no more on the matter." *But I wanted to!*

"Ha! Well, that makes two of us. Walk the plank or call me when *you've* grown up." She ripped the top hat from her hair, and I watched as fiery locks spiraled down her back and over her heaving cleavage. The girl tossed her hat at my feet before yanking the door from my grasp.

"I need a number for that!" I shouted as she drove away. The peal of tires cut off my retort.

No more banter. No more ball-busting bitchiness or susceptible softness, sweet perfume, coconut-scented lotion. No more cinnamon on her breath near my lips. *No more Anne Bonny and Calico Jack!*

I cursed the empty silence while my eyes drifted to the ground. *How to proceed?* She wanted proof, action over words. Impossible for too many reasons, but if I failed to act, someone else would, or worse, she'd ignore my wisdom and run back into the arms of someone who may have attacked her in his need to have what she'd refused. *Did he stand her up before or after? Or had someone else attacked her after she'd been stood up? Why would she protect them?*

Who the hell cares!

She's gone!

Gone!

Why did she matter?

Was I a bloody masochist because she made my palms sweat?

After long years on the job, nothing rattled my cage. She not only pried at the bars of my prison but sent an earthquake through the very foundations, setting free the possibilities of life. I was so bloody screwed.

I grabbed the hat and dusted off the brown felt. A burst of bay breeze carried her scent from the accessory. Instead of emasculating myself and lifting the perfume to my nose, I trudged to my Range Rover to drive away from here and this experience. Eric was likely waiting at the storage shed while I was playing bloody games with a girl.

I opened the door as a shield, yanked the gun from the holster at my back, pulled back the hammer, and spun to take aim on another pirate.

"Freeze!"

"Shit! Easy, King!" Joey cried. My personal protective detail's hands flew up beside his temples. The feather on his cavalier hat waved in the wind. My barrel poised two inches from his face, but he whistled with the wry grin of a card sharp holding a royal flush. He may as well have been. He had enough to run to my superiors and out my interlude with the girl.

"You're mighty brave, mate." I lowered the gun and thumbed the safety in place. "Lucky you didn't come any closer."

Joey dabbed sweat from his brow. "I'd say you're the brave one. She's mean. Aren't you lucky I caught these in case you needed a witness?" He held his phone up as I holstered the Sig. His display lit with several images of Bitchy Bonny flaying my heart. I masked my excitement. "She looks cute and harmless," he said, "but for a second, I thought I'd need to step in and defend you. Especially when you armed her. She has the coat. The coat has the knife."

"Maybe I prefer a fair fight," I joked. In truth, I was glad she kept the weapon in case she needed to castrate whomever left the prints on her arm.

Joey chuckled as he emailed the photos to my inbox, then deleted them until arriving at the final picture.

"The good news is...drum roll please...." His thumb scrolled. Kinsley's license plate centered on the screen. "Guess you got that number after all."

Regret replaced with promising reprisal as he sent the photo then hit delete.

"Ready to go hunting?" he asked.

My lips spread into a villainous smile. "Damn right."

CHAPTER 4
KINSLEY

Coach Walton roared across the track, "Faster, Micro Machine!" My spikes dug harder against the rough texture. "Dammit, Kinsley! Where the hell is your sprint?!"

The girls beside me gaped as we ran across the finish line together. I glared. They looked elsewhere while I swiped an arm over my forehead to curb the sweat dripping into my eyes.

The women's track coach inspected me, but allowed Ian Walton, my personal coach and trainer, to dole the scolding while she focused on the hurdlers.

"Kinsley Hayes, you *see* this garbage?" The vein between Walton's eyebrows protruded from his red face while he shoved the stopwatch too close. "This is NOT scholarship timing! Any high school superstar could outrun you! What am I doing here?" He threw his hands and the question out to the rest of the team.

"Great question since I'm not going to the Olympics!" I tossed back. Walton ripped the hat from his head and held the brim as he pointed at me.

"Keep up the attitude and see what happens," his voice dipped.

"That a dare?"

"That PMS?" He placed the cap back over his sweaty hair then gripped his hips and waited for me to pop off again. I forced my lips into a thin line. He nodded his triumph for having the last word and sauntered to the water cooler. When I growled, three fingers waved over his shoulder. I cursed and gripped my knees. He may as well have flipped me the bird.

My father watched from the stands, having taken the afternoon off from work to offer motivation. Without looking, I sensed him jogging down to 'coddle' me, though I wanted to be alone with my angst. Instead of waiting for him, I changed into cross-trainers and started the three-mile punishment Walton had flipped me off with.

Daddy joined in the next lane a moment later.

"Kinsley Fallon. This isn't like you." Both names. Yay.

"Want to talk about it?"

"Nope." I pushed faster, forcing him to speed up to punish him for his concern.

"This about Valentine's?" he pressed. He didn't stick his nose in my business when he figured I'd come clean on my own, however, today his nostrils seemed brown. "Nate didn't get you anything?"

Ha! Unless the rose tucked beneath the windshield wiper on my car was his idea of resting a flower on the grave of our relationship. "No."

Nathan wasn't worth mentioning or speculating about, and he seemed a minor issue with the new chaos scrambling my thoughts.

"Daddy, I suppose it should be, but this is about me growing the hell up."

Dad winced at my curse. "I'm not sure what that means."

"Don't you?" I gazed at him in accusation, ponytail slapping my shoulder. Unfair, but in my current mood, I resented that he'd raised me to expect better of men. What a crippling fairytale. And I must appear a fickle child if he figured a lack of Valentines from an ex could turn my sprint to crap. *Couldn't he be honest?*

Daddy ignored my tone but quickened his pace in retaliation. "Didn't he apologize?" He metered his breathing. "It's not like him to leave you hanging. Perhaps he had car trouble? There must be a reasonable explanation. He wouldn't just abandon you."

"No car trouble. Julie saw him park at his frat house just fine. It's been three weeks since he stood me up. How obvious does he have to make it before you'll accept it?" I asked between controlled huffs.

"He hasn't called or texted?"

"He apologized in a lame voicemail, said his plans changed. Given his silence, I realize his plans with me have changed."

My father said a Christian curse under his breath.

"It's not the end of the world, Daddy. *My* plans have changed, too. I'm not stopping at my Bachelor's. I'm going for my Master's. Screw giving up my original goals for a jerk lacking the balls to break-up with me."

"Easy on the vulgarity, Kins. Love isn't sacrificing your dreams. They can co-exist. Just because he wanted to get married doesn't mean dropping out. He might've lost his nerve."

"Lost his nerve?!" I screeched to a stop. Daddy halted and tugged my elbow, which I effin' hate, so we were out of the way. "*Marriage?*" The word tasted like Dial soap in my mouth. *Hadn't matrimony been what I'd daydreamed of only a month ago?* "Does it appear that he was thinking of proposing?"

"Well, I think it was a reasonable step after over a year

together. And...." He worked to form words. "Nate loves you, Kinsley. He's a good man. It makes no sense for either of you to give up a great thing over one missed date. Forgive him. *Fight* for him. I don't understand your defeatist attitude. It's out of character, even if he upset you. You're not a quitter."

"Pft! Fight for him? Forgive him? No. I'm not quitting. If something is finished, let it be and move on." He looked stung, but how did he think I felt? He had my mother and a white-picket-fence relationship, the freedom to entertain romance. My generation seemed intent on murdering what remained of men willing to work for a woman's attention, not to mention the women who still made them. If he learned the true reason Nathan stood me up, the danger Nathan had led me into, I doubted he'd push the issue.

"It's simple," I said. "Nate doesn't have what it takes. He's a coward. When the right guy comes along, I'll fight for him. Until then I won't awaken love before it so desires. Shouldn't *you* be spouting this?"

"I'm sorry, honey. You seem...*different*."

I was *different*. That pirate had effed up my entire world when he'd called me to the carpet and revealed the type of alpha male I'd thought had gone extinct to really be an endangered species.

How had a stranger ripped to shreds the relationship I'd viewed as perfect the day before Gasparilla?

Psychoanalysis didn't punch a dent in reasoning why the encounter haunted me, or the rationality of co-mingling fear and attraction. The less sense this made, the more I tried to make up a sensible explanation and the more I obsessed about the pirate. This was ridiculous, but psychological definitions had nothing on a host of undefinable sensations. My whole Psychology major seemed upended, like seeing photos of a roller coaster and reading a person's account of their rush.

Coming away from those things thinking you're an expert on their experience because you've studied the evidence to the fullest."

When the pirate had lifted me to my feet, gripped my hips, tugged me close enough our chests touched, caressed his thumbs against my waist, looked ready to kiss me...I'd fallen down the first rapid drop before several loops and corkscrews and now walked in the shoes of the roller coaster rider with the disheveled hair and huge smile, lingering butterflies and nausea in my belly. Whether I rode the ride again wouldn't erase the experience and the craving to get back on. Not once had Nathan's full kisses made my toes tingle or knees weaken the way the pirate's touch had. Never before did I have the desire to kiss a stranger. I'd like to blame heartache and near-trauma for a lapse in good judgement, but was that fair?

Nothing about the encounter lined up with the person I'd created myself to be. Now, I thought of my every action and reaction compared with my peers'. I thought of my standards and questioned whether they were too high or low. Picked myself apart to be someone better than before. Wondered what made me a kid versus a woman in his arrogant, condescending eyes. *Why the hell would my body thrill at such an attitude problem? What the hell was wrong with me?*

Dad eyed me, and I realized I'd spaced out.

"I see why your trainer is angry. Something more than Nathan is bothering you, and your sprint is suffering the consequences. I'll respect your privacy, but I'm always here. Don't harden your heart again, baby. You've come so far."

I sighed in defeat, knowing I wouldn't hold out for long before confessing. We didn't keep secrets. "I hate crying, Daddy. Bitterness is easier. Give me some time. I'll come around."

"If that's what you need, I'll give you space."

"Daddy, is there a man with a British accent where you work?"

"What?" His brows crinkled the space between his eyes. "Not in my office."

"I mean in the building."

He chuffed. "Companies from all over the world do business in that building. Not only British, but Japanese, German, Chinese, Spanish—"

"Never mind."

"Why?" He gave me a suspicious once-over. "Is this the something more than Nathan that's bothering you?"

"Remember that space you said you'd give me? It commences now."

His eyes combed my face. I'd known better than asking, but the curiosity killed me.

WORK, school, track, repeat.

For the next two relationship-less, dateless, lackluster years, I received zero calls from the pirate who'd told me I was wrong. Apparently, I'd overestimated his intelligence. After all, my top hat had a full *if found please call* tag under the inner elastic with my phone number. You'd think a man brave enough to arm me with a Bowie knife in the pocket of his pirate coat would've reciprocated and inspected the only accessory I'd given in exchange.

Whatever. With him, I didn't want to be correct. The realization sucked, and I held it tight to my chest. Every time I went to my father's building, I hoped for a man to walk by wearing the cologne from the coat. Several times I had, but the hell if I could pin the fragrance to one person when the coffee shop was always crowded.

Instead of love or lust like my friends, I found my adrenaline in winning races, climbing the ranks, and amplifying my moniker's reputation. When I wasn't training, interning, or studying, I lost myself serving Jack, Jameson, Jim, Johnny, Sailor Jerry, and ignored the lasting image Captain Morgan left in my mind.

In the here and now, I looked at my fellow bartender, Bayleigh, and asked, "What cocktail does Frat Toy, here, look like?"

She giggled at my label for a regular flirt who frequented weeknights.

A group of his fraternity brothers gathered at the bar around him, each of them awaiting drinks based on our evaluation of their personalities.

Bayleigh narrowed her eyes on a hot one and began her assessment.

"Kamikaze, baby. This is for you."

The headliner slapped money down, interrupting our playtime. He licked his lips, and they lifted at the corner. "Sorry, guys." Jase Taylor was a lot of things, but sorry was never one of them. He gloated because they hadn't a shot in hell at hook-ups when he was in the building. Bayleigh and I seemed the only two he didn't aim for. Jase assessed the group as I pushed his drink across and thanked him for the tip.

"Thank *you*, sweet Kins." He kissed my cheek to spite them. When he pulled back, Jase focused on the frat brothers while I feigned indifference. "You boys keep your hands to yourselves, ya hear? Would hate to schedule a meeting with you in a dark alley after work."

"All right, Jase. You've made your point," I told him.

"You're welcome." He grinned, zero shame in scaring them away. "Any song requests?" he asked as he picked up the drink.

I cocked an eyebrow. "How about ..." my finger tapped my chin. "*Cold Little Heart*?"

That got a hearty laugh from him. If Jase had the choice, I'd have empty pockets and no dates.

"That your boyfriend, Micro Machine?" Frat Toy asked as Jase headed for the stage. I giggled at the absurdity.

"No way. He's my best friend's older brother. She's attending FSU. When she's away, he extends the relation," I explained. "He's home on leave, but y'all better do what he says, because you don't want his trouble, especially in Kamikaze mode. There's a reason I dubbed him with that drink."

They weighed my seriousness and whether their pride was worth defending.

To distract them, I leaned close to Bayleigh again and dubbed the frat boy of choice, "LIT and make it strong." He nodded his approval like I'd given a flirtatious compliment. She chuckled at the inside joke. Long Island Iced Tea was almost all liquor, but in my experience, the drinkers always requested I make theirs 'strong' like they had something to prove.

"We'll all have one on me, but water theirs down. The pledges can't handle their alcohol like we can," hot guy said. His buddies laughed, and throughout the evening honored Jase's threat, aiming further flirtation at Bayleigh. None of them asked me out, but not only due to the hulking singer hiding lethal skills greater than performing the panties off patrons. Rumor was, 'Micro Machine' was scary on the track, therefore undatable.

Rumor also was, Jase Taylor might be home for good this time.

In that case, I'd better prepare to be a poor old maid.

CHAPTER 5
KINSLEY

As I trotted into the bar, I dodged cat calls from the day-drinking veterans and snowbirds playing cards and dominoes.

"Tell Marcus we approve of that new uniform, Kins," one teased.

"Yeah, yeah, go for the full house," I told a veteran, peeking at his cards in passing. He cursed and they folded while I rushed to the register behind the bar to clock-in.

"Hey, powder puff," barked a voice box full of gravel. "Make me a proper Rusty Nail when you get a chance."

"Mm-hmm," I hummed and pounded the buttons harder than necessary. A glance over my shoulder, I regretted agreeing before assessing the Inferno biker sitting at the bar. He needed cutting-off.

"Thanks for coming." My manager strode from the hallway and paused to stare. A dumb whistle followed. "You look ...."

"I don't want to hear it. My uniform is in my locker. When Mommy has a tea party, girly dresses the way Mommy wants or else she might have to move out and pay rent."

He chuckled and splayed his palms. "What? You look hot. Mommy needs to have more tea parties before I call you in early."

"Marcus."

"Not the dress, but the rest, yes, please. Taylor's gonna eat his balls for breakfast when he sees you this way."

I rolled my eyes at his referencing Jase. Marcus wasn't going to butter me up. "Had to skip track practice *and* teatime with my mother and her frou-frou friends...." I trailed off and looked up into his face, pretending I wasn't thrilled to be relieved of the obligation. Too bad I couldn't have changed clothes first.

"What's the delay?" The biker slapped the bar. I no longer feigned irritation.

"I'll make it worth your while." Marcus lowered to a whisper. "Water his drinks down after Sara leaves."

"She's still *here*?" I asked in kind. *Why was this a secret?*

"In the back with a friend of Taylor's while she grabs her stuff."

I finished with the buttons and looked at him like he was the crazy one. No one goes in the back but employees, and what was one of Jase's friends doing here? Jase wasn't even on the clock to perform for a few hours, and they all knew Sara was married.

"He offered to walk her to her car. Given the current audience, I'm cool with that. Feel me?"

"Marcus, is her son sick, or was I called in because she's bailing on yet *another* shift? I hate being lied to."

He sighed. "Name your price."

"Really?" He knew what I wanted. I quirked my eyebrows.

"Dammit, Kins, you know Valentine's Day is always packed."

"I can clock-out and leave you till my real shift begins.

After all, winning doesn't happen on its own, and my mother was threatening to vis—"

His hand chopped my voice. "Deal. Find someone to take your shift that day, though. I don't know why you don't want all the extra tips, and you know you'll be spoiled with gifts. Girls love junk like that."

"Mmm, most girls love junk like that," I corrected and walked over to the liquor counter. Pretending to stash my clutch, I grabbed an empty bottle of Drambuie from the recycling bin and slipped the new one behind the fluff of my dress, swapping the full with the empty. "Think you can handle this long enough for me to change?"

Marcus rolled his eyes and waved me past him to the hall, where I handed off the bottle. "Brilliant move, Little Red. See why I need you?"

"Right." I paused before the hallway to peer at the biker. "When I'm in uniform, I'll make you a fresh drink, okay?"

He nodded. The veterans started a new round of cards while I promised them a fresh round when I was changed.

At the end of the hallway, Sara pushed through the door to the rear parking lot, a man following. I couldn't park back there today because of my stupid attire. Gravel and heels don't mesh well.

I sighed after stuffing the froufrou dress inside the locker. Either her son had a new immunity issue, or Sara was hiding something. She'd been flaky for the past three weeks. Since I was the only one available on short notice, I took the hits.

"Oh, come on!" I pleaded, ready to boot the lower locker with my stupid heels. Since I didn't go home or to practice first, I didn't have a spare set of tennis shoes. My toes were already complaining. This was going to be a long shift. *No good deed, eh?*

I stuffed my arms inside the top to stretch the Lycra as

much as possible, but the fabric molded back to every curve. I spun in the mirror to see my back in the reflection and shook my head. "This is too risqué for off-season," I muttered. Even when we had to wear heels when Spring Break hit, I skated by with platform wedges. "Ready for a new type of unwanted attention, Micro Machine?"

"Red heels go great with that new embroidery," Marcus goaded in open appreciation a few minutes later. He smiled at my deadpan, knowing how I hated I couldn't remove a name tag to swap the new shirt with a larger size.

"If my parents ever catch me in this, they'll kick me out into the real world, and I'm blaming you."

Marcus's laughter faded as he disappeared into his office. When I moseyed behind the bar, I noticed the biker's heavy eyes fall like anvils to the high heels.

"Oh, no," I whined and produced the biggest innocent eyes I was capable of. His face changed as I turned the empty liquor bottle upside down trying to pour a drop into his cup. "Marcus, do we have anymore Drambuie?" I yelled.

"Are we out already?" he called back. "The next shipment won't be in till Tuesday."

"Looks like you cleaned us out, sir." I shrugged with empathy. "I'm sorry. You come in tomorrow, and I'll make you a proper Rusty Nail. Deal?"

I never worked Tuesdays. He'd be Marcus's problem.

The wasted biker wavered on his stool and stared like awful things ruminated in that mind. My palms tingled as I evaluated the room in case this guy did something stupid.

The cowboy who'd followed Sara through the back door now leaned beside the digital jukebox in a pair of vacuum-sealed Wranglers. A flosser churned circles between his lips while he, too, watched. He tapped the touch screen a couple times, and I stifled a laugh when his song selection began, the genre opposite his appearance. His voice joined Nick Jonas's to provide comic relief. He sidled onto a stool beside the biker, singing *Chains*, rather well, by the way. His radiant eyes followed my movement as I made a till for my lap apron.

The biker's slow stare bent to consider the cowboy with disdain. He called him a foul name, then stumbled off the stool, curses about our bar and staff flooding from his slurring mouth all the way out the door. *Thank you, Jesus!*

"It's a shame he had to leave, eh?" Country flirted, pausing his idiocy.

"A true shame." I nodded and tugged the tap to fill a pitcher of beer for the vets. "Seemed a sure thing among the oldies, but I guess I was wrong."

He chuckled as I went onto the floor to deliver orders and clean vacated tables littered with empties. The best way to keep in touch with town happenings was to listen to old men gossip, and the moment I bent to wipe a table, I hit pay dirt.

"That hick right there's gonna get himself tangled in a nest of vipers flirting with Sara, now Kinsley," one old-timer said to another. "Everyone knows whose turf this is. I don't have to agree with 'em, but Nightshade takes out the trash."

"Yeah, but they're all criminals."

"Now, Ned," a snowbird said. "You know the rumors just like I do. Nightshade been dealing Oxi to the locals like Robin Hood. You can't tell me after being busted up in our youth, we elderly don't need something to kill the pain of old age."

"Yeah, not to mention the memories," a vet added. "Don't know about y'all, but the only nights I sleep are through thunderstorms and fireworks. Can't handle the silence. If I take a little sumptn' sumptn' to help me sleep, where's the harm in that? Not like the VA came through."

"Lower your tone, brother." Another vet took a watchful

survey of the sparsely populated space. "I'm clean, and I happen to like my VA benefits. I prefer to keep them."

"Pft. Only because they legalized the devil's lettuce in your county and you know how to pass a piss test, otherwise you'd be the same level criminal as you accuse Nightshade. Besides, not like we're sniffin' or cooking somethin' on a spoon or shootin' syringes and what have you."

"Shhh, seriously, what're you trying to do? I get your point. Nightshade's not Inferno, but I don't think we should be talkin' so openly. I came to enjoy myself, not get involved in another useless battle. Damn." He slapped his cards face down and leaned far enough back that his chair teetered on its back legs.

'Ned' shrugged. "Marcus don't care. He knows the difference between the way Nightshade conducts their company versus the company Inferno keeps. And maybe after all the useless battles, I have a hard time sitting idly by in my old age seeing blatant sex trafficking without consequences. Slavery. Right here, right now. Bad may be bad, but at least Nightshade don't sell humans. Hell, to some, we're the villains for slaying villains overseas, and that's about all I'll say on that."

The one who'd laid his cards down sighed and crossed his brawny arms over his chest, took another look around, eyed the blond on the stool at the bar. "Sara said she had trouble with Inferno. Creep wore a vest like the guy that just left." He lifted a thumb and pointed to his chest. "*I* think that was one of his friends hunting on his behalf. Trouble flocks together."

"Like us," a quiet vet added while thumbing through his cards. The lot laughed like a knife through tension.

Ned said, "You ask me, the Infernos are a disgrace to fire departments and bikers everywhere. A gang of firefighters who can't control their hoses, spraying corruption on the good reputation of honest emergency responders. Ruins the whole system."

"Greed, politics and bad actors always do," a quiet oldie said in bitter wisdom. "Selfishness is the root of all evil, and the men in those vests care nothing for saving any lives but their own."

"Amen, brother. Then you have these girls holding their lives in their hands when they work jobs like these in uniforms like those."

A stern finger pointed right at me. I hated when they talked as if we weren't in the room, or like we were 'asking for it'. Guess in their minds men had no control over themselves in the face of cleavage? Although I agreed with their views on selfish desires and the trashy reputation of Inferno. Interesting perspective on Nightshade, although in my mind, wrong was wrong.

"You're lookin' mighty pretty today, Kins," the older veteran told me, sheepish for the trash talk I overheard.

I bent to retrieve his glass. "Thank you, sir. My mama made me look like a proper lady, but I don't think these heels convey in this uniform quite the same as they did with my dress. Since I got called in before I could grab my tennis shoes, I'm stuck marching like Minnie Mouse." I kicked up a heel. He and his pals exchanged glances and nodded. I almost pressed them for details on Sara but decided to mind my own business. "Don't y'all go getting me into trouble with my daddy for it either." My gaze met the eyes of the guilty parties one at a time, and I earned a salute from a Vietnam cap.

"Yes, ma'am."

A pair of shriveled fingers from the Korean cap handed me a dollar bill to keep. My smile came like he'd gifted five dollars, and I traveled back behind the bar. The singing siren on the stool spun to face me again, a new song playing that I crinkled my nose to. He scoffed and stood like I'd issued a challenge. My head shook as he went back to the juke box.

"Hey, girl. This here's musical communication at its best." His smile radiated hayfields and sunshine, while his cocky walk in those tight jeans spelled a certainty in his ability to get into any girl's pants he desired. He'd best take those snakeskin boots out the door if he thought to aim for my panties.

"Hey, *boy*, how many guys do you think we get in here trying to serenade us with that machine? And if that's the best, guess I'm left with something to be desired."

With a call of my name, the corner table lifted their empties. I dug inside the cooler for a couple Buds.

Country ignored my tone. "Worked, didn't it?"

All right, he had me there. "It did. Thank you."

"If you don't like *Chains*, what do you like ?" He squinted to read my name. Or gawk at my boob. Hard to tell which. I covered the embroidery. "Ah, come on, that's not fair. How will I order from you?"

"I don't take orders, I make them." I grinned while several veterans lifted their hats and nodded their approval. Barn boy howled with a hand over his heart.

"Quick on your toes, ain't you, Red?"

"You might say that."

"Was that your sister?"

"No."

"Better be careful. A man may confuse the two of you in dim lighting, flirt with the wrong woman."

"That's what she's got *me* for, Jarhead." Jase Taylor's voice boomed as he walked into the bar from the employee's hallway with the swagger of a champion boxer ready to deck a challenger in his ring. "This perv giving you a tough time, baby?" His honey irises glazed my face before squaring up on the stranger.

"Hey, Squid, I don't want no trouble. She wanted a song. Gotta give the girl what she wants if she can't get it from the singer." *Oh, hell.*

"Now I *know* you're full of shit." Rather than throw a punch, Jase's hand clapped loud against the blond's, and they pulled each other into a guy hug. *Whaaat?*

"Kins, put a round for them on my tab, please?" a veteran asked in a one-eighty shift from his previous disapproval.

"Sure. Um...anything else?" This made no sense until I recalled Marcus saying this was Jase's friend.

"Yeah, you keep these boys in pain, ya hear? Don't let either of them steal your virtue."

I laughed and saluted the man in his Vietnam cap the way he'd done me. "Yes, sir. No worries there."

"She always knows precisely where to aim to take a man down a couple notches," Jase joked with the veterans as he and his friend traveled to the table to thank them for the drinks.

"Ah, son, be grateful for the dose of humility," the veteran teased. The group shifted into acronym style military speak I didn't comprehend, but Blondie's fluency proved he was a military man who now claimed his flirtation with Sara and me was a diversion against the bikers.

When Jase walked back to the jukebox, the blond said he was trying to find a song that depicted *Red*. "Did you realize there were twins working here, and *you* didn't tell me? Two stacked redheads and nothing but oldies to entertain them? You've been holding out."

Jase's laughter filled the space. "Why do you think I called you?" He winked over his shoulder while I rolled my eyes, then he turned back to his friend. "And *I'm* not old. Sara isn't natural. Kinsley is. That's Red's name, and you don't choose a single tune for this one, she's too colorful. Why do you think I'm here singing twice a week? Always hunting for the right song." He grinned in my direction, but I resumed wiping the bar.

He asked the vets for requests, and one called out a mixed drink. Jase selected non-committal blues tracks for them, then glanced at his friend. "Gotta set the tone before I set the stage. The band should roll in soon if you're interested in singing some blues."

They claimed the stools across from me. Jase removed his cap with the flourish of someone who could just as easily remove his burdens. He laid the hat between us and leaned on his muscular forearms just as I left to deliver the drink. "Butter my damn biscuits." His eyes shot to the heels, then traveled slowly back up as I pretended not to notice or hear.

"You want your norm, sir?" I rounded behind the bar and posed against the polished wood knowing he would do his best to focus on my face. Even if he'd just checked me out, he cleared all appreciation as fast. This horn dog didn't mind his manners with anyone else. He played, but kept me at a distance, then allowed sluts to climb all over him on performance nights. This was a rare moment of female monopoly on his attention.

"Meh, I'll do beer later. What's your read today, baby? Do us both." He grinned, one side of his mouth tilting up. Jase could stop the pacemaker of an old lady's heart with that grin. I licked my lips, then gnawed my lower in contemplation of Jase's current assertiveness. His lips mimicked mine, but his silent gesture baited like a lure tossed into a lake. Was this his bestie's influence?

"Hmm...." I grabbed the top shelf vodka since the band wasn't on the clock yet. Jase would have to pay for his own drink, and I'd make him pay for false flirting. After shaking the ingredients in the tumbler, I faced them and poured each an expensive shot, then slid Blue Ribbon cans beside them, snapping the tabs with a smug mug. "Kamikaze shots and cheap beer, gentlemen." My empty hands found the edge of the chunky wood surface and held tight like I could hold onto this faux confidence the same.

"Aw, I don't get anything different?" Jase pouted.

"Not when you refuse to change," I quipped. His friend held a fist over his grin.

"The cheap beer is different, what're you trying to say, Kins?" I didn't answer, just tapped my temple and smirked.

"Well, Rusty, I see you've made a lasting impression on my future wife." Jase grinned at his friend.

Gimme a break.

"Or mine." The friend grinned back and pulled the flosser from the corner of his mouth. Meh, at least he didn't have a cheek full of chew.

They clinked shot glasses in a toast, then downed them in tandem. Country boy hummed at the flavor of the shot, then winced when he sipped the Pabst. "Should go down on one knee seeing you make him pay for his pain, but something tells me you're the type to take it slow." He winked. "Rustin Keane, at your service, Miss. Pleasure to meet the one woman Jase *can't* have." His smile beamed radiant and clean. His free hand gripped my own in a shake I respected. No jelly. He returned the sentiment. "Firm grip. Nice." Rustin's eyes smiled as I rolled mine and made Jase another at his request.

The bell jangled over the door while I pushed Jase's glass in front of him. They turned to study a biker vest striding up to a stool. "Well, well, well. Kinsley. You're here early, darlin' and looking mighty fine!" He ordered a draft, and his fingers danced bare from the tips of leather riding gloves in a taunting wave at Jase. "So is tonight's jester. Wonder why." Silence expanded between the five stools separating them.

"Because I asked my favorite *headliner* to keep me

company," I lied, knocking this perv down a notch. Jase quirked his eyebrows at him, then cast his smile at me.

"Where's Sara?" the biker asked, all business.

Rustin piped up before I could answer. "She had to leave."

"What's it *your* business, corn-fed?" he demanded.

"She'll be back tomorrow," I offered to stifle the brewing pissing match. "Want peanuts with this?"

He glowered at the guys for a long moment as he decided whether to pursue his issue. *What was his issue, though? What was Sara's? Dear, God, please don't tell me the vets were right, that she's tangled with Inferno.*

"Yeah. Sounds good." His gaze roamed my body. I didn't have to look. I felt the disconcerting sensation when I bent for the nuts beneath the bar, wanting to twist his in my fist and hear his pitch rise in panic.

"You should come in early more often, Kins. Wouldn't hurt my feelings or my eyes none." My skin crawled as I slid the bowl to his chest, then grabbed a towel to begin wiping tables.

"Don't count on it," I told him as I walked away from the bar. "This isn't my crowd."

I'd only been here for an hour and hated day shift already. *Why was Sara doing this to herself when she was the star who'd trained me?* None of this made sense with her character.

He whistled and cursed as he twisted on his stool to watch my advance on a vacated table. "'Specially in them shoes. Could stand to see you and Sara together again. Tips must pour in when twins are on duty."

"Ugh, why does everyone keep saying that?" I muttered. Sara was four inches taller, ten years older, two cup sizes larger, and had a good fifteen-to-twenty pounds on me. I wasn't trying to be a snob in my own mind, but I didn't work out for twenty hours a week to be compared to someone who barely did.

"Who said I was meaning you and Sara?" the jerk asked.

I discreetly wrapped my fingers around the neck of an empty bottle. Jase didn't miss the movement.

"That's enough." His stool scraped across the wood as he stood. The veterans lowered their cards. "Kinsley, say the word, and I'll deck him." He didn't look at me, though. His gaze trained on the biker in ways that went deeper than this one instance. "It'll cost ya lip action instead of that cheek tonight, though."

"If he keeps it up, I'll do it myself, and you can kiss my cheek for doing you a solid."

"Everyone wins." The biker grinned at my threat, his glance prancing over the bottle in my hand. He tapped his cheekbone to show where to aim. "You hold his leash? I always assumed it was the other way around."

"That's it." Jase moved, but Rustin did, too, like a man bent on diffusing a bomb, to block his friend. His eyes warned me to stay put and ease my white-knuckled grip on the glass.

"Jase, he's not worth spilling blood Kinsley will have to clean up." The anger in Jase's eyes held and trained on his friend's face while the biker snickered. "Save it. Go prep the stage." Rustin's voice remained level. Jase's eyes shifted to mine for permission. I subtly nodded. He did, too, then resigned and patted a watchful veteran's back as he went to the stage.

"Yeah, go play with your instrument," the douche poked. "It's all you're good at."

"Hey, he's not the only one. If we're keeping score, *I'm* the best at beating off!" Relief hit as Jase's drummer, Mel, slapped the A-hole's vest in greeting, then wove his tatted arm around my waist. His pierced lips warmed my cheek, and his mouth drew close to my ear. "Someone needs his ass kicked. You okay?"

"I'm fine. Glad to see you. Is Marcus back there?"

He nodded and drew in again. "The rest of the band is out back unloading the trailer, but we scoped three other Infernos in the lot. Marcus's out there keeping score and making sure the one doesn't drive drunk." *The other one never left? Creepy.* "I'm gonna make a phone call so Jase doesn't get dirty. Sound good?"

"Damn right."

CHAPTER 6
KINSLEY

The snowbirds and vets trickled out. Twenty-somethings mixed with middle-aged patrons as the early evening crowd filed in. While I looked for cops or Mel's connections, Jase's irritation simmered down as his local fan base filled tables near the stage. Rock-N-Awe's Blues gig drew crowds to this place on Monday nights, but their Thursday night Alternative performances produced twice the turnout. This crowd spelled great things for the upcoming tourism season.

At the far end of the building, Jase's buddy aided the band in setting the stage, making small talk with the other members and curious barflies. I marveled at his ability to keep Jase in check and make him smile again. Jase's sister, Tyndall, might be envious, and I itched to call her and ask about him.

Bayleigh clocked-in, then shuffled to my side to catch up on orders until she spied him across the way. "Who is *that*?"

"His name is Rustin. From what I've gathered, he's Jase's old bestie from some out-of-state po-dunk town. With a twang like his, I'm guessing Texas or Alabama."

She hummed her lust. "A twang to match those jeans? You know I love a country boy. Is he part of the band?"

"As in, will he be a regular weekly appearance?" I asked. She gave a giddy nod, and I shrugged. "No idea."

Garrett, the other bartender on shift, clocked-in and scoped Rustin with narrowed eyes lined in Urban Decay thicker than my own. He wound his thumbs beneath a set of red suspenders and snapped them, the definition in his biceps flexing with the movement.

"Straight?" he asked. His chin lifted as he grabbed a rum bottle, tossing and catching it behind his back for the ladies. Garrett always made that flair look easy.

Bayleigh beamed, seconding Garrett's question.

"Oh, yeah," I said. "He's straight. Keep rocking that eyeliner, bud. Your buns are safe."

We giggled, and Bayleigh leaned against the liquor counter, ogling Rustin unraveling cords he plugged into amplifiers. "See how TDH handles those cables. Bet he does wonders with rope."

"Bayleigh! Shame on you." I grinned. "Should be TSH."

"What do you mean? What's the S for?" She smiled.

"Instead of <u>T</u>all, <u>D</u>ark, and <u>H</u>andsome, he's Tall, *Stupid*, and Handsome. He would flirt with our mop if we convinced him there were boobs somewhere in there."

She cackled, earning gawks from a group that bellied up to the bar with an open tab. "All those boobs are paying him ample attention, though. Makes sense," she told me as she scooped ice. "Bet you he crooks a finger and they come running to save a horse. I sure would," she admitted. I chuckled at her allusion to a popular 90's country song. After doling refills, she cupped her chin in her palm with a girly sigh. I knocked her elbow from beneath her. She snapped out of her appreciation and shot a glance at the hallway.

"What's up with Marcus tonight?" she asked.

Between mixing drinks, I filled her in on the biker's behavior and the Rusty Nail who came before him.

"Okay, uncomfortable, but it's not as if we don't deal with bikers, and you know anyone with testosterone is going to test Jase's. He's too muscular for Neanderthals who want to see who has the biggest club." She backhanded my abs and nodded at where Marcus stood. He had both meaty arms crossed over his chest evoking the bouncer he used to be. "He looks extra pissed. Did the guy actually scare you?"

"Meh. I was more nervous about Jase wasting his energy on a bark with no bite. Just another scuzz, ya know?" I shrugged then turned to thank one of the bar-backs for lime refills. She nodded and echoed my thanks.

A guy in a Tampa Bay Buccaneers cap muscled through the cacophony. "Coke. Cherries on the bottom, grenadine, please, love?"

"I've got it." Bayleigh filled the Brit's order while I poured a quick row of shots.

"Now *that's* an accent, woman!" I told her without looking at the Brit at the bar. "The other's a slower form of speech so TSH's mouth can compensate for his brain."

"Brutal!" She giggled and tossed Garrett a towel when there was a sloppy spill near the end of the bar. The night was shaping up to be busy, but I found my eyes following our manager more than the musicians. Bayleigh made a good point. Marcus gnawed his toothpick hard enough he could shoot splinters at the next person to piss him off.

I leaned in on a free moment. "It's possible Sara had an issue with Inferno that made her leave early. The oldies were here gossiping about it earlier. They mentioned a vest, but you know how the rumor mill goes. Don't quote me on that."

"Makes sense, though." Bayleigh cringed and peered at Marcus. "Two Inferno assholes in one day?"

Maybe her kid wasn't the sick one ....

"Wonder what Nightshade thinks about it?" she mused.

"Excellent question." We tried to spot Nightshade members surveying the damage. Unnerving, because members were difficult to discern, but I'd be willing to bet that phone call Mel made was to someone connected since I didn't see a single cop in the crowd.

"No way they aren't involved somehow," she mused. "Turf wars are ugly. Let's hope the scumbag keeps his hands to himself. Marcus looks ready to throw punches."

We shared a knowing glance. He had to restrain himself anytime an Inferno jangled the bell over the door since they had their own bars. Inferno came for the pure enjoyment of causing a stir. For the time being, Marcus was talking with the guy Bayleigh said she'd just served. "Oh, Kins, did you see him?"

"Who?" I asked, distracted with drinks.

"The British Invasion! He was so TDH."

I scoffed and shook my head, rarely the double-take type of girl.

"You should have," she said. "It's the perfect contrast: Rustin is Neutrogena clean like pure sunshine, but the *other one* is dark and broody like he's shrouded in moonlight. Damn hat hid his eye color though. Wonder how Marcus knows him?"

"What do you mean?" I asked and garnished a pair of mojitos with mint sprigs before passing them across the bar.

"I mean Marcus is chatting with him like they're familiar."

When Marcus caught us staring, the man's head snapped our way as if we'd shouted his name. "Yikes," we said in unison. "That's our cue to deliver drinks."

We loaded a tray full of the band's faves, and I lifted the heavy disk over my shoulder to begin the bumper car trek through the crowd.

"Check. Check. One-two," Jase chirped into a microphone. His fans clamored for seats and tables like a mad game of musical chairs. Those at the bar held mugs and bottles up with shouts and cheers. Jase took his stool at the helm of the band as they settled into their places and tuned instruments. "Thanks, baby," he said as I set the tray near his feet. I turned for more drinks, but his sharp whistle pulled me back. "Kiss, please?"

Jase swung his guitar to the side to dip down toward me. I angled my cheek, prepared for the familiar warmth of his cushy lips and the scratch of stubble. Instead, warm fingers curled around the nape of my neck, and heat prickled the corner of my mouth. My eyelids fluttered closed on a deep inhale. My head tilted against his hand. Tingles shot through my chest depriving my lungs! *WTH!*

"Do I get one next?" Rustin's voice sounded too close.

I opened my eyes and pulled away, determined to pass drinks around like all was chill, controlling the release of my breath. "Ha! That's his for good luck. Our kiss is ritual. *Not free.*" *And, not normal.*

"Guess I should start singing, then." He smiled. I had the uncomfortable urge to back up because of how near he stood. I smelled his cologne, saw up close the fine lines at the corners of his mouth, the variations in his vibrant eyes. His pale hair enhanced the bronze tan on his skin. He snagged a brew off the tray and handed the bottle up to the bassist. His arm hadn't needed to brush my breast. Jase reached between us and cupped my cheek to thank me and reassure that he would have a great night. *Who was this guy and where was my best friend's brother?*

"Yeah, you better." I smiled at him and turned a 'kiss my butt' glare on Rustin. He propped against the stage with a bottle in hand and held eye contact with a smile in his eyes as he took a sip. *Give me a break.* "You guys signal when you're empty."

Jase teased the strings on his guitar, his tatted-up bicep and forearm flexing with every tantalizing stroke. He nodded, and his gaze rested on mine longer than usual, like he was doing math in his head. I tilted my head, puzzled by why Rustin's flirting with me didn't bother him, but everyone else's did?

Was he wondering about his glitch in kissing so near my mouth, too? Worried I'd fall all over myself and ruin our friendship with his mistake?

Meh, I had orders to fill and no time for dwelling.

Drink requests shouted my way at the same rate song requests were thrown into the large Mason jar at Jase's feet. Greenbacks colored the band's tip jar beside the requests, and my pockets filled well for an offseason Monday. The band's cover music became the soundtrack to my work while they warmed up. Jase made a game of prodding men to call out songs for their significant others, ones that got away, or 'bitches who'd broken hearts.'

Bayleigh applauded when one came in for her from a regular with a crush. He loved the pain, she loved shooting him down, then picking him back up. This was fun. The same fun that kept me from quitting on the bad nights, or the nights when I felt guilty for all the skin my uniform showed.

"I'm tagging someone else in," I told the bartenders when at last I returned behind the bar. "I need a breather."

Jase finished another song, then dug through the papers in the request jar. "Hold, please!" a nearby voice shouted.

"Hmm...what might *that* one be requesting?" Bayleigh hummed with a finger at her lips. Marcus's friend waded through the mayhem waving more than a few dollars in his hand. Jase joked with his band mates about big spending.

As the guy reached him, Jase leaned down and whistled when the wad of cash and written request exchanged hands. "We've got ourselves a high priority tune, ladies and gents." Jase's eyebrow lifted as he read the title. He looked back at the band like *you've got to be kidding me*. "No wonder you gave me so much scratch for this, man. Gonna make me go there? I may have to kiss that bartender again to resuscitate my masculinity." The crowd laughed with uncertainty, and I grinned on a wave of my finger. He was very flirtatious with me tonight. Made me curious. "I'm gonna bring in the extra help of my way-back-buddy, Rustin, who knows this song much, *much* better than I do."

Rustin hopped on-stage, showing as much curiosity as the rest of us, but introduced himself with a country flourish and took a mic and guitar from the nearby stand. The audience welcomed him before he leaned over to hear the song title from Jase.

"To be clear, does that say what I think it says?" he asked.

"That it does, my friend, that it does...." Jase trailed off while Rustin guffawed. *Hmm.* "Think you're up for it?"

The duo shared a nod and warmed the horde with small talk while they adjusted instruments. Someone from the floor offered Rustin a stool of his own. Marcus was in my ear, checking to be sure I had nothing to report. I tugged bottle caps in quick succession while downplaying my earlier discomfort.

"We need you safe, all right, Little Red?"

"Safe from what, Marcus? Perverts? What else should I expect with the new uniforms?" I shrugged and flashed a bright smile. He ignored my dig and didn't buy my blasé explanation. I focused on the band to dissuade him from pressing for more. He delivered bottles to the barstool patrons and cut me slack.

"Hey, man," Jase called out to his requestor. "Who is this for?" The patron's muffled voice broke through. Jase snickered, then came back to the mic. "He says it's complicated. Did you break her heart?" Everyone struggled to hear the response. "Ah, someone else did. He endured the fallout. Hey, we're here for you, boss. Marcus ought to make sure you aren't attacked in the parking lot if she's in here somewhere." The entire place erupted in laughter, me included. There was another muffled exchange. "She's *here*? You've got balls of *steel*, dude."

Everyone looked around for this mystery woman, wondering if this would end in a happy reunion or a drink tossed in the brave soul's face.

"Who is Complicated Moonlight, and does he do therapy sessions for broken hearts?" Bayleigh mused as she toweled beer foam off her hands. Jase looked over at Rustin as they worked out the notes to a song that had the masses in riotous laughter. Jase's huge smile stole his ability to get the first lines out.

"*Big Girls Don't Cry*?" she snorted. "Fergie? That's messed up."

"Agreed." I giggled.

She pulled her phone and went live. "This is happening. Keep an eye out for claws about to mar his pretty face."

I choked on another laugh when I caught Jase zeroed in on me. Bayleigh didn't miss his focal point, either.

What the hell?

He closed his eyes to belt the chorus.

"Is it disturbing that Jase knows these lyrics and notes like he does this one on his own time?" She ended the recording and tucked her phone back into her pocket. I smiled, but what was up? Shouldn't that offend me if he was staring at me while singing that song?

"Holy crap, Kins! Are the claws *yours*?"

"Huh?"

Bayleigh snatched my reach for a liquor bottle. "Moonlight! He's looking over here! What if it's for *you*? Do you know him? What's complicated? Did you break down and punish him for it?"

"Ha!" But as soon as I laughed, she shook me as if I held information she needed to save the world. Breath whooshed between my lips like a pregnant woman in Lamaze. "No way...." Peering where she insisted he was, I didn't have a clear view of the man she'd dubbed Moonlight. He was back-lit. His face was a mystery. *But, what if...?*

It's complicated.

I'm complicated.

"Nope. No. No. No. Not possible," I told myself. *A British accent! Oh, hell.* "Wait, didn't somebody call me love earlier?" *No one with an accent had called me that before the elevator or since! Until tonight!*

I wanted to rush out into the crowd and rip the hat from his head! To glimpse the face that haunted my decisions for the past two years without the veil of a costume! The asshole who was just dick enough to come to my job and call my childish crap even still! *He recognized me?*

When I skirted around the bar, the man vanished, and I spun until connecting with Jase's hawkish eyes. *What was happening?* I sensed turbulence, although everything appeared the same on the surface. The hidden undertow scared me. Jase was deeper, blatantly flirtatious, and that kiss had been the furthest he'd ever dared. Rustin seemed to be pushing Jase's envelope. Three men in competition all at once. Two passively telling me to grow up. One doing so from his screwed-up sense of humor, or who the eff knew?

Before the song ended and Bayleigh interrogated me, I

collected my things and clocked-out for the night. Thank God I'd taken an earlier shift! I raced to my car like I could outrun the questions sprinting through my mind at the pace of my heartbeat.

Was I imagining things, or had the pirate I'd assumed walked the plank just resurged from the depths to call me after all?

CHAPTER 7
KINSLEY

Five a.m. came too soon.

I tumbled out of bed desperate to punch the lights out of the snooze button. Ugh. By five-fifteen, I'd risen from the dead, clad in a sweatshirt and track shorts, secured my hair in an ugly bun, and double-knotted the laces on my cross-trainers. The bun jostled with my lethargic steps to the kitchen. I covered a long yawn while my left hand fumbled inside the cupboard for an energy bar.

"Come on...dark chocolate...peanut butter...not fruit chalk...." I played my tiny lottery. Dunno why I always bought the gross ones.

The luck of the draw, I suppose.

With a banana and a water bottle tossed into the mix of essentials, I shouldered a small knapsack and trotted down the stairs to my car. The brisk sting of cool air jolted my eyes wide open with a rush as effective as a cup of coffee. Psh! The thrill of the pirate coming into the bar to call me back to the battlefield lit a fire beneath my feet.

En route to the beach, my thoughts replayed the unforgettable interlude two years prior. Was the pirate handsome without his costume, or plain but influential in that way you don't notice he's not attractive? One thing I did know, he was ballsy and knew how to make an entrance. He also had the best cologne in the world, along with a grip that reeled in my attitude despite casting others further away.

I swallowed some water and fished for the power bar.

"Hell, yeah! Today's forecast is...." I drummed against the steering wheel when I bit into a peanut butter bar. *Oh, happy day!* "Thank you, Jesus." I turned up the music to force my head out of pirate-shaped clouds and into the frame needed for a five-mile jog before the obstacle course.

Familiar lamps brightened the sidewalk like the warmth of an old friend's smile. After parking across the street, I killed the ignition and got out to savor the rumble of waves, salty breeze against my face. I closed my eyes through a deep breath and opened them to survey the deserted obstacle course sitting to the right. I gathered my water bottle and phone, locked the car and coiled the keychain around my wrist.

Though dawn threatened to nudge the moon from its lazy haze, buttery light floated over the gulf, reflecting with the shimmy of the currents. The waves ferried beams ashore then retreated into the spray. Damn Bayleigh. Moonlight would never shine the same. He might not be that pirate at all...what if he were actually the man I'd kissed at Julie's murder mystery party last year?

I concentrated on my warm-up, stretching before hitting the sand, but contemplated kissing that stranger and how the thrill felt versus almost kissing Jase. Ugh. I didn't want things to be weird at work or make him feel like he had to mansplain his mistake like I was one of his desperate groupies.

Rather than insert earbuds and drown nature's solitude, I jogged in the ambiance that paused all else on my brain, the continuous rush of water, seagulls fighting for fish while plover and ghost crab dodged my footfalls in their quest for periwinkles beneath the sand. No competition here. My rare quiet place.

Will I maintain my GPA until graduation? Eliza's times weren't as sharp when I'd hurdled beside her. Please, don't let her be mad at me.

Is Jase into me, or am I reading too much into things? Dammit! The same things I just said he shouldn't have to worry about! If I asked Julie for my murder mystery make-out partner's name, maybe I could ease Jase back into the same safe place he'd always been. Would he remember me?

What had Sara flustered enough to change to day shift? Did Inferno have her inventing excuses to leave? Was she in danger? Was Rustin warning about someone mistaking me *for her?*

Shut up! Quiet place!

Just me and the run. Just me and the run.

I veered further from the shore to where the sand wasn't as firmly packed. The difficulty of running in powder silenced all thoughts of anything other than the pain of the push against the resistance. My breath steamed in hot, even pants as I trekked past each lifeguard post. When I turned around at the two-and-a-half-mile mark, or ten lifeguard stands along, the sun crested above the horizon to the east. My favorite part, something only a few other early-bird joggers and I shared as I soldiered toward the obstacle course.

Sunlight painted the sky in orange sherbet. Distant barges illuminated against the horizon's infinite edge. The gleam of metal monkey bars stole my attention as I neared phase two.

Finishing with a full sprint, my heart thrummed like a

snare in my ears as I pitched my water bottle into the sand and huffed onto the obstacle course.

Today was my first morning back since last semester. I expected to be rusty.

'I swear, you'd be so strong with a real man.'

Get out of my head 'Moonlight!' Screw needing a man to be strong!

I bolted through the tires with the fervor of a starving cheetah racing after a gazelle. Slinking up the rope climb, across the monkey bars, I ignored the raw pain in my palms. At the pull-up bar, I squeezed out seven, then bounded up the large net and warred with the swing and sway as the braided nylon threatened to toss me off in front of a couple of voyeurs drying their faces with towels. At the top, I lunged over the block wall the net secured to, stuck the landing on the other side, and proceeded to lather, rinse, repeat. As I leapt to the ground a third time, a guy stretched at the tires, dark hair, expensive sunglasses and workout wear, a sleeveless tank showcasing definition (despite the chilly temp).

His routine differed from mine. We didn't cross paths often, but at the pull-up bar he eased himself up a dozen times as though he could've asked me to pick a number, any number. I forced my pride and noodle arms to strain through another seven and ground out an eighth in spite. Even as my muscles trembled when I dropped, I gave myself a fist pump. *What a great morning!*

He smiled before running to the rope while I sped to the net again. Causing his smile made *me* smile, too, especially since his demeanor conveyed a thread in common: he didn't seem to be one to entertain fools during a workout. Neither was I.

This guy was fast, because soon he was on the net. The

ropes rocked harder as he rambled past me (and my pride) with an effortless vault over the wall. I touched down behind him with a new surge of determination. My reward was an impressed nod that in no way delivered credit because I was a girl.

The victorious adrenaline I loved propelled me into a bonus lap. Wasn't he kinda challenging me to workout *with* him?

This time, however, two more men occupied the equipment, and my challenger force-fed me his dust for breakfast. *Dammit!* I fell behind, but pushed myself harder to prevent having my buns whipped by these other beasts.

I drove harder as I shimmied down the rope and jogged to the monkey bars, following another attractive torso across, though his hair was blond and matted with sweat.

While I wondered where the dark-haired guy went, I now dreaded that stupid pull-up bar. Humidity compounded with the sunrise; the metal was nasty and slick when I jumped to grasp the bar. My fingers slipped off. Strong hands arrested my fall and lifted me like a child to regain a firmer grip. Before I popped off, I turned and looked over my shoulder. *Jase Taylor!*

"Morning, sweet Kins." He nodded with a smug grin that read my accidental attitude loud and clear, then cranked out pull-ups beside me. Since this was a bonus round, I did three and left him there doing—well, I lost count after eleven. The other guy made them seem as easy with his James Bond build as Jase did bulging like Captain America.

Grateful he didn't try talking through the workout, I pushed that sculpture from my mind and ran to the net. My turn to give an appreciative smile when Jase landed right behind me.

I left him and huffed over to the shorter bar for core work.

My sweatshirt rubbed like a Brill-o pad against my sweat-stung skin. I shrugged from the stifling sleeves to peel the drenched collar over my head and tossed the discomfort to the sand, then chugged the remaining water from my bottle. Although the air chilled the soaked tank to my body, I was overheated. Several men roamed the beach shirtless, and two ladies jogged in sports bras for the same reason.

An old treasure-hunting couple wandered close to the shoreline to sweep a metal detector over the sand and collect pretty shells. I focused on them as I gripped the bar and hooked my knees over the dew-dampened metal, dangling upside-down to make my abs scream. After pumping crunches well beyond exhaustion, I dangled. Rays of sun glittered against the soft waves, a pair of pelicans above coasted on the breeze. Sand Pipers skittered around the old couple as they sought periwinkles beneath the sand. The metal detector beeped and scattered the tiny birds.

I smiled as the old lady bent over. The man nagged her about letting him do the digging.

"Nonsense," she griped. "You just want the credit when we find the Spanish gold."

"Woman, I know how to share. Been doing this for over fifty years now, haven't we?"

She waved him on and stood with annoyance that didn't convey in her smile.

Adorable.

I wasn't sure how long I let the scene steal my thoughts, but I startled when a hand waved in front of my face. Jase cast a disarming grin, his elbow propped on the bar. A bare eight-pack, protruding biceps, and popping pecs gleamed with perspiration like a freshly waxed car after a sun-shower as he combed his fingers through sweat-soaked hair.

I dismounted to stand before him, squinting against the sun.

"Hey!" I breathed. "Thanks for the help back there. The pull-up bar was kind of slimy." I cringed. Inside, I face-palmed at the thought of him singing that I be a 'big girl now'.

He chuckled. "Agreed! Wonder what *nasty* jerk spilled his fluids without cleaning up?"

"Oh, it's the dew."

He glanced over his shoulder. "We should blame Rustin," he whispered with a thumb pointing to the obstacles.

"Ha! That's gross, but deal." Figures cocky Country was who I'd admired on the monkey bars earlier. Good thing he didn't earn a vindicating look to inflate the ego he sported.

"Did you guys have fun last night?" *Why did you stare at me while you sang that song? Did you know the requestor? How does Marcus know him? What about almost kissing me on the lips???*

"We did pretty well for an off-season Monday." He seemed casual enough. "Although, it just wasn't the same after you left." He winked and peeked again over his shoulder. "I think I watched the fire go out of more than a few of the men in the room, including Rustin, when you walked out the door, especially in those high heels."

"Aw, not you, though?" *Crap!*

"Yes, *me*, too. That's a given, sweet Kins. I don't like when you work early because you leave early. My muse," he sighed with a pearly grin at the Heavens. "People throw food at me when you aren't working. I wish they'd pick something softer and tastier. I hate broccoli, but at least it fed the horse's ass over there." He snickered and tickled my ribs.

My cackle burst louder than I wanted as I jumped back. "I'm sure you both had partners waiting in the wings to cheer you up."

How bizarre to have his open attention. The only things thrown his way were bodies, bucks, bras, and bikinis. You better believe he made a lot to headline at the bar *twice* a week, and he turned dimes to dollars in our pockets with every show. *No complaints here!*

"FYI...." He leaned close like we shared a secret. "No company but each other's last night." He waggled his eyebrows and another embarrassing too loud laugh joined with my slap to his sweaty arm as my flirtatious alter-ego presented.

"Ah, the gay card. Makes sense why you've never asked me out." *Mouth diarrhea! Abort! Abort!* I didn't want my heart broken when he confirmed *any* reason. Hell, I didn't want my heart broken at all, and Taylor Street was a one-way lane of heartache only the moronic traveled.

His grin faltered. *Ugh. Brace yourself. Stupid Kins!*

"Wait, what?"

Come on! "Well, you know, you flirt a lot, but...." I gulped, begged my nerves to calm. *Did I even want anything?*

For goodness sakes! What had I done?

While I panicked inside, he tugged at both ends of the towel slung around his neck and chewed his lip like *he* was the nervous one! *Whoa!* I had never seen that expression on him before!

The brilliant blond jogged over and broke up the awkward moment. Jase seemed relieved and disappointed at once. I felt that.

"Damn, guys, I'm happy to see you, too." Rustin panted. *How had I not recognized him?* "You, Red, are a *tough* woman." His beam framed a deep set of dimples as he tossed his chin toward the course. "That normal for you?"

"Affirmative."

"How come I haven't bumped into you before?" Jase

asked, glad for the change in subject. "I'm always here for lifeguard training."

"That's right. Tyndall mentioned you were a lifeguard. Maybe lifeguards aren't the early risers I am," I teased. "Can't force dedication." He rolled his eyes, so I slacked up. "Just playing. I hate when guys come onto me or women give me the death ray because of my drive. I try to wake up before the perverts and haters. True story."

"Makes sense," Rustin said. "Although, I don't think perverts adhere to time constraints. It's kind of a twenty-four-seven preoccupation." Rustin squinted at me, then fired a grin at his buddy. "Better keep your eye out."

Jase's hands came up in surrender. "Hold up. Did you think I was hitting on you? Because I wasn't. I was just being friendly. Can't cross paths and not say hi. That's rude." His lips clamped shut at Rustin's sigh. "You come out here *every* day?" Jase wondered.

I fought the sting in my cheeks at his admission.

"Not *every* day, but when Track season is upon us, I'm here every opportune morning for extra conditioning." I supplied an invitation I shouldn't have written.

"That's right, Tyndall mentioned you were a runner." *Touché.* "We're about to jog down the beach. Want to join? In a platonic, friend-zone sort of way?"

Rustin nodded beside him, a dangling tongue the only thing absent from this dog's mouth, hope dancing in both sets of eyes like wagging tails. *Good grief.* Last night, I'd booked out to avoid them in my confusion. Today, I'd clipped leashes to their collars and given them names!

"Sorry, guys, I get my run in before the obstacle course, and I have class. Another time?" I had no classes today, but big girls had more to do than flirt with boys, and apparently, I'd read too much into Jase's everything. Not like I wanted anything. *Sigh.*

Best to bolt. When they expressed their regret and pleaded, I smiled and turned them down. *No more mixed messages today, thank you very much.*

I plucked the nasty sweatshirt from the ground and shook off sand as I walked off the beach. To my surprise, the guy— workout clothes guy—granted a polite nod from behind his ever-present sunglasses as he, too, made his way toward the parking lot.

I fell into distant steps in the same direction as the first guy to workout with me on the course. The silence expanded with my mute plea for him to talk to me. I'd sworn-off dating, but how vindicating if Jase saw that maybe I *hadn't* thought he was coming onto me.

"Impressive pace on the course," I prodded before we reached our vehicles. *Come on, dude! What am I missing?*

"Ditto."

I inhaled. I loathed that word.

"Ditto, huh?" I uncoiled the bracelet from my arm, unlocked my Civic catty-cornered to the Tesla he cruised up to. His head rose. I longed to smack the sunglasses from his eyes to see them when I called him out.

When he smiled, not the same smile he'd given before, suspicion and familiarity collided like flint and steel creating a spark. This one enjoyed a private joke remarkably like the man who'd followed me to my car in that parking garage two years ago. *The same arrogant asshole? No effing way! The pirate used 'ditto', too!*

My heart drummed, but my pride shouted louder.

I cleared my throat and anxiety, noticed the similarity in the way he carried himself just the way the pirate had. *Well, hell. Here goes.* "A minimal effort word from a *man* who outperformed me on the course? I'm disappointed, and had you asked *today*, I would've had coffee with you. Nothing too *complicated* about that."

Boom. Mic drop.

A gorgeous smile cracked his catalogue-model-cool. If he *was* the pirate, how fabulous to be driving away from him again? If he was not, still awesome to demand a guy man-up.

The fan of my fingers as I drove away was a crap-calling bonus.

CHAPTER 8

KINSLEY

Open mic night crawled at a sloth's pace. Thanks to Sara, Marcus called me to work a shift I'd long-since sworn off.

"It's my night off." I balanced my phone between my shoulder and ear as I tossed my duffel bag into the backseat.

"Little Red, I need you. Sara can't make it and Garrett and I are unloading the truck. Even if it's slower than the other days of the week, Bayleigh can't man the bar and the tables at the same time."

"What about bitch-server?" I asked and got into my driver's seat, started the car.

"Really?" Marcus' speech broke while Bluetooth connected. "...has a name. It's embroidered over her chest. She has her second job and can't work Tuesdays."

"I hate open mic night. What do I get in return?"

He sighed. "I'll give you Valentine's without having to find a replacement. If I have to work your shift myself, I will. Deal?"

Though the Hallmark holiday loomed a couple of weeks away, who could say no to that? The confusion swimming through my mind over the guys was enough without the added

71

anchor of turning down gifts and invitations to go out with men I'd not trust to feed my mom's cat.

"Deal," I said. "We'll shake on it when I get there."

An hour later I rubbed a condensation ring away from the lacquered bar.

Tonight's patrons buzzed low and laid back without touching the mic. We listened to the juke on free play and helped Marcus tick off inventory. For now, the biker I'd promised a drink to hadn't shown, which was nice. Bayleigh and I kept up with orders as Garrett refilled coolers with cases he hauled from the back. A bar-back refilled the trays of cherries and wedges of limes, lemons, oranges. He tossed us the ugly cherries to snack on. I worked the stem of one in my mouth with a smile as I thought of men trying to impress us with their knots.

The toe of my sneaker tapped along to the crooning of *Bad Moon Rising* like a cheerful omen as Moonlight bubbled into my head while Marcus simultaneously asked about Blue Moon bottles. The iconic sound of CCR faded while I traded Fogerty's voice for Jase's.

Two men on my mind at the same time. On top of that, I hummed along, picking apart Jase's and Rustin's odd dynamic on the beach this morning. *Were they competing for my attention?*

"Both dogs chasing the same ball, but the one to catch it first can destroy it all by himself? What do you think?" I asked Bayleigh after the replay. She called the Blue Moon count to Marcus. He asked Garrett to bring a case. Bayleigh double-checked the fruit arrangement as the bar-back replaced the lids over them. I spat the knotted cherry stem into the trash.

"Meh. Jase's crush on you is the worst kept secret in town," Bayleigh said and checked the olive bin. "Whether you're plain blind, or off-limits due to your code of ethics, I can't figure out, so neither can he. I say keep him confused till he makes his intention obvious." Nausea soured my gut. *Was she right?*

"And Rustin?" I asked. "It's weird. Where does he fit in? And why?"

Marcus took the case of Blue Moon from Garrett and strode behind the bar. The bottles jostled as he set the box on the bar, then flexed his bulking bicep to make us laugh. "Rustin could be the final straw, or Taylor's excuse," he injected. "He's close to making a move. I'd bet money on it. Seeing you all prettied up yesterday must've got the caveman going with all the competition. I keep trying to tell you, wearing heels might take you off the market."

"Ha! Sir, you need to hush."

Bayleigh and I shook our heads but smiled.

"True story. Pretty legs in a set of heels, a little skin—"

"A *lotta* skin." I called his crap with a dry edge. He never paused.

"—will make a man ignore a butter face all day long. And if she is a butter face, that vanishes with each passing shot. It's a win-win for the bar."

"You should be ashamed of yourself," I told him.

His turn to chuckle. "You'll never have that problem, Little Red, so my advice is maybe leave your options open?"

"Thanks, but what's that supposed to mean?"

"It means," Bayleigh intoned, "he *knows* Complicated Moonlight. And that even if you grow old and fat, you'll be the opposite of a but-her-face. Your face will be pretty when everything else fades. You'll be a butter body." She cheesed and elbowed Marcus for holding out.

He studied her like WTF while I laughed but thanked her.

"Hold up. Complicated Moonlight?" Marcus asked.

"Yeah. The crap-calling song requestor from last night. The Bucs hat." *Buccaneers. A pirate.* "Admit it, he requested that song for Kinsley, didn't he? You're doing the chummy guy thing where you watch out for your wing man, and he's doing that thing where he pokes the girl with the stick, so she'll smack him. You never forget the boy that pulls your hair and pokes ya."

They all snickered as I shook my head in disapproval, but what a thrilling idea from a man who had decided I'd been too young on our first round in the ring!

Garrett weaseled in to tell Bayleigh to catch the order at the end of the bar. "You want the rapid low down in real guy speak?" he offered with a gleam in his eye. "Jase is a slut in love. Rustin is a redneck pervert. You two invent stupid names for patrons, and your TDH has come in sporadically over the years, but more often lately, enjoys Michelob or Captain and Coke with cherries and grenadine. But when you're on-duty, Red Running Hood, he usually leaves or settles for cherries and Coke. He either wants to control himself around you or avoid you. Think he suspects you're the wolf?"

"Garrett! You brat!" I cackled, but everything came to exhilarating life at the idea that he'd been under my nose all along. *But why wait all this time to reignite our sparring match?* "What's his name?" I asked. Neither man spoke.

Garrett cleared his throat and glanced at Marcus for a beat. "I lied. TDH is here for Jase, and Jase is in love with him. Rustin is the jealous lover come from afar to stake his claim before all is lost forever to some childhood sweetheart." His forearm covered his forehead like a damsel in distress, while I gaped at the terminology pertaining to my role. "Thus, ended the fantasy of every bartender working last night and praying they might be a big girl now. Don't you remember about fifteen other women sitting right in front of the bar? You guys make this too easy. Ooh, speaking of TDH...." Garrett's voice trailed with his eyes as they followed an exotic Latina model-walking toward the stage. He rubbed his hands together and wished us well with our PMS and angst. "Looks like she needs instructions for the mic. I'll whip you up some chocolate martinis when I return."

Bayleigh and I stared him down while Marcus called, "Take your time, Garrett. These things can be complicated!"

Garrett grinned over his shoulder. "You know it, boss."

"See what I mean about them heels, girls?" Marcus jeered. We exchanged a look. Marcus was watching out for bros before hos, confirming her point.

When he asked about the liquor bottles, we gathered the almost empty liquor bottles and used them to assemble trays of dollar shots, then yanked the pour spouts. Marcus went to grab the new bottles.

Bayleigh proposed, "Next time they come in, I'm feeling the situation out. Pass the lime wedges?" I grabbed the bucket and pushed them her way. "Thank you." She arranged them for the server who came to take the tray. "I'm hearing a lot about Jase and Rustin, but you're suspiciously quiet about the one I'd go for, which makes me think you'd also go for Moonlight. It's okay to admit, at least to me. What's not to like? He's mysterious, older, and *not* Jase." She and Jase equaled two sluts of the same feather with little else in common and a sibling rivalry dynamic. "Or maybe you *should* pick the dude who serenades you while every other woman, besides me, envies you through your oblivion. Kind of feel bad. Jase's certainly tortured himself long enough over you."

"Ugh! I hate this!" I stammered. "He doesn't serenade me. If you can't even make up your mind, how can I be expected to? Forget it. Graduation. Internship. Track. Grades. My IQ is dropping by the day."

"Right. That new internship you're hoping for might be great when you get it, but can it make you—"

"Bayleigh. Pass the bonbons because I'm not listening to your sex talk. Jase is a fool if he makes a move. Same with Rustin. And if Moonlight is older, he's worse than them. No one will ever stay faithful because they'll be too busy cheating with hookers to be in a celibate relationship. Let's not go there."

"*Au contraire, mademoiselle.* An older one has the restraint that a younger guy doesn't. If they've got their junk together, they can keep it together. Their wild oats are sown. They recognize there's more to the savor rather than devouring a quick bite. Assuming *you* can stay celibate, he may not have as hard a time waiting...."

I chewed my lip in recollection of the things the pirate said to me before I left him in the parking garage. *Hadn't he implied something similar? Was that part of why I ought to stop dating little boys and opt for men?* Jase and Rustin weren't exactly boys anymore. Jase was almost thirty years old.

Before hope turned me into a girly idiot, I forced myself to remember there was a great divide between words and action. Jase had years of inaction to show, years where he even relegated me to his friend zone.

"Celibacy is for pussies who can't close the deal," a crass voice barbed. I turned to see the dreaded biker walk up to take a stool. *Ugh.*

He eyed the new bottle of Drambuie while I peeked at the time to see how many hours I'd have to endure his BS.

"You didn't think I'd forget, did you? You promised me a drink."

I hated drunks who retained memory.

While I set to work on his rusty nail, Bayleigh walked around the corner to, I assume, grab Marcus. The biker's deceptively kind smile lifted from my butt to my reflection in the mirror. "You ever been on a motorcycle?"

I cocked an eyebrow. "No."

"That singer have a bike?"

"Not that I know of," I told him, trying not to show exasperation. I saw where this was headed. "Last time I checked, to join a pissing match, you have to be a shoo-in for the competition. Bikers aren't my type. No offense."

"I'm not offended." Seemed true enough, but that gleam in his eyes soured my gut. "I can't fault you for your inexperience. Like sex. How can you judge something you've never had? Who doesn't appreciate the lure of a virgin? It's like pay dirt. Especially to that singer."

Ouch! Was that why Jase put me in the friend zone?

My cheeks stung and I over-poured his Drambuie like a nervous novice. He noticed and chuckled.

"Besides, you think you want celibacy, but *you* need a bad boy to keep the worse boys away. Your singer talks a big game, but he's weak over you, and that makes him weak. Period. Bikers can be scary when they need to be."

"Bikers can also be nice rather than creating a poor image for the rest," I ground out and slammed his drink on the wood before him. "And you know nothing about the singer. Back out of my business or leave the bar."

"Well, well, well...." He took the drink and gulped the entire thing in three swallows, then mimicked how I'd slammed the glass, making me flinch. "Maybe I was wrong." A slow smile took over a sinister undercurrent I hadn't spied till staring at him. "That weak singer could use someone like you to keep him safe."

Safe from what? Last I checked, SEALs didn't need the protection ....

I jumped and squealed as the bottle of Drambuie shattered near my feet.

"Damn. That was the only bottle in this shipment, Kins."

Marcus cursed and bent like he was cleaning the mess. I hadn't even realized he'd walked behind me! When he stood, he had the neck of the broken bottle in one hand, his empty trash bag in another, but there was zero missing his threat. Bayleigh tossed the biker's glass in the sink, then crossed her arms over her chest as she stared at the pervert.

"What a shame," the biker said. He made a show of duck lips as he considered the liquor bottles. "Rusty nail ain't my only drink. Good thing there's a whole bar. How about...a Blue Moon. Bottle, not draft. Careful how you hold that, man. Looks like a threat."

Marcus held his gaze and nodded. "Yeah, you're right." He shoved the shard inside the bag. Garrett picked that moment to come back. The pep in his step faltered somewhat when he took in everyone's expressions and body language.

"You asked for a Blue Moon? Did I hear that right?" Garrett chimed, diffusing the static. "Bottles are still warm. I'm gonna tap the draft, okay? Hope you don't mind plastic."

"Yeah, that's fine." The biker grinned right at me like he knew something I didn't.

What the hell?

"Kins, since it's slow, you have bathroom duty," Garrett told me while he placed an orange wedge on the cup. I nodded and grabbed the mop, wanting to throw the wood like a stake into this vampire's heart.

In the bathroom, I glanced at my reflection to see my cheeks alight. Turning the tap, I scooped some cold water to pat against them, then stared back at myself to talk my nerves down.

Bayleigh came in a second later. Her hand soothed over my back as she searched my reflection. "Don't listen to him. Not all men are whores. Your singer is weak for you, but I think Jase keeps that guy afraid to misbehave the way he'd like to, and that's why he's pissed."

"Sometimes I really hate this job."

"No, you don't. You hate perverts. If every biker were like him, you could hate it, but you know most of them are good guys wanting to look dangerous in their leathers." We both smiled, me reluctantly. There were some adorable men who came in feeling like a million bucks with their swaggers and their *ol' ladies* beside them, even though we'd seen them two nights before in collared shirts discussing stocks and golf games. She was right. That part I did love. "Don't let one jerk-off and his trashy gang ruin it for you."

"Thanks, Bay. I don't know why he rattled me."

"We both know that Jase sleeping around bothers you. Unfortunately, it's not hard to unsettle a good girl about something that would naturally upset her." She scooped my hair over my right shoulder and bent to rest her chin on my left. Her blue eyes met mine in the mirror. "Jase isn't the only option. Just for you, next time Moonlight comes in, I'm knocking that hat right off his head and unmasking him. Would you like that?"

I rolled my eyes, but my cheeks grew warm again as I nodded.

"I'm going to prove that it's all shadow illusion. That he's unattractive in the daylight hours. No booze. No shade. Male pattern baldness is a good reason for the cap. I feel much better now. Don't you? Glad we had this talk." She clapped her lips shut and smiled. I reached up and cupped her free cheek, then turned my head to kiss the other.

"Thanks for helping with Inferno. You're a good friend, Bayleigh Blue."

"Thanks. Just don't tell anyone. My reputation will be ruined." She moseyed to the door, pausing as she grabbed the handle. "At least if Moonlight's unattractive, you'll have an easier time narrowing a winner."

"Pretty is as pretty does, Bayleigh. Looks aren't everything."

She chortled at the ridiculousness on her way out. I took a long look in the mirror, thinking of my morning. If he proved to be whom I'd suspected earlier, Bayleigh might knock me out of the way to take him on herself. Memories of his athleticism had me ready to run away to a convent to hide. What was that saying about corrupting a nun?

God, help me! I prayed and started mopping.

CHAPTER 9
KINSLEY

For the next two weeks, school poked along while not a single guy worth flirting with came into the bar. Fortunately, not an errant biker did either. Work was blissfully boring in that regard, but a dangerous restlessness had taken root. Existence in a classroom with my nose pressed to the glass lost some luster. Had there always been this many couples mingling around campus? Had I gotten so used to wanting to gag myself at their public displays of affection that I'd ignored them altogether?

The days passed in a blaze of dedication but lacked adventure. Didn't matter if I blocked out Bayleigh's sex talks. My mind was captive. Not by the act of sex, but the anticipation and subtle hope that a worthy partner may be riding over the horizon. Even the flavor of victory during meets needed spice. Nothing compared to the adrenaline rush I'd enjoyed the night Complicated Moonlight made a request of the man Bayleigh swore was serious competition for him.

Was he brazen enough to make another request, or would

he turn out like the wussy guys I sat near in today's Color Theory course? They tossed glances, but never met my eyes.

All little boys, love.

Mr. Miller, the *one* adjunct professor that demanded we call him by his last name, owned the only set of XY chromosomes in the place that made eye contact without shying away. A man. Also, the only professor who didn't treat his students like petty subjects begging at his throne of wisdom and precious time. I got the impression he did this job as a hobby more than survival, which might explain his evident enjoyment versus those so pressed to pay the bills they exhausted themselves teaching almost twenty classes a semester.

The errand boy from the staff office wormed his way into our lecture, delivering flowers and gifts while the girls reacted like an ATM spewed free cash.

Crap! My throat dried. How had I forgotten Valentine's Day? I *hated* vulnerability, and I *hated* that I had no reason to get roses from anyone but my father.

Still...

Shushing my inner girl, I refocused on the awful slides projected up front. The art professor's poker face was worth the course. I didn't need the class. Jase's little sister, Tyndall Taylor, was an Interior Design major. To better understand my best friend, I'd opted to appraise ugly art in an attempt to see the same beauty she insisted was there. Wonder what she'd think of Miller and his slides of the most ridiculous canvases. I snorted to myself. Tyndall would be too mesmerized in checking Miller out to notice the slides.

Meanwhile, these minions attempted to impress him with feigned sophistication. Pathetic. He knew they were brown-nosing and exploited their ass-kissing like a bonus sociology lab. I rolled my eyes.

"Ms. Hayes, your opinion on this piece?" he called my crap.

I considered the single yellow line in the center of a black canvas that unjustly made the big bucks.

"That's easy." I smiled to cover my embarrassment, glad for the dim lighting.

"Oh?" he asked. A snobby jerk from the table beside mine stared to see what *I* could *possibly* contribute. Okay, not everyone avoided eye contact.

"Yeah." I gestured to the screen. "That's a light saber. Although, the artist should have made the handle easier to spy. Luke's great, but I'm a Han Solo fan myself. Add a classic Harrison Ford somewhere in there to liven things up. Some Chewbacca fur to give this extra texture. *I'd* be ready to mount that baby on the wall."

Miller tossed his head on a pleased laugh, and the class followed suit, except for the snob. This was serious business.

"Interesting perspective considering this piece predates the era of *Star Wars*. Perhaps the artist was a time traveler?" Miller teased.

"May I?" the snob asked, righteous indignation all over him. Miller nodded. "You see—" Snob gestured toward me, then the slide. "—this symbolizes the light beyond the door closed off to the darkness of the world."

Several students hummed and the class shifted to deep thoughts of the shallow minded. Why he'd singled me out, I wasn't sure.

"Ooh, I like that," I admitted, unfazed. "Although, if the door were completely closed, the light would emanate from the bottom, whereas this yellow stripe is vertical, therefore the door is cracked open. The question is whether the person in the dark is pressing the door open to peer into the light, or vice versa?"

Another hum throughout the student body. The snob sneered. Miller spoke up. "How very Hermann Rorschach, Ms.

Hayes, Mr. Anthony. Each piece, much like an ink blot, is subjective and dependent on your view of the world."

"Always have to outdo everyone, eh, Hayes?" the snobby Mr. Anthony whispered as he leaned into my personal space. "Maybe we'll get lucky, and you'll sprain an ankle this season."

"Aw, is that a bruise on your ego, Anthony?" I grumbled under my breath. "Or just the shadow of the demon living inside your black heart?"

"If it is, are you gonna grab your Bible and perform an exorcism on me?"

Miller cleared his throat and shot us a warning look. The sting went all through me while Anthony wore an innocent expression.

"You know, class, art is also a fantastic tool for mature dialog on differing perspectives with exceptionally low risk for personal threats and name-calling. Therefore, should you encounter such a virulent art critic, consider ousting their toxic temper or else your perspective may become tainted by the same poison."

Damn! My eyes bugged at Miller's passive aggressive threat as I stared at the table.

"In conclusion, Mr. Anthony, did the artist's child cause a happy accident on his father's canvas, or was this simplicity created on purpose to expose us as the deep-minded frauds we think we are? The world may never know, so each one of you are correct. Next." Miller clicked the remote in his hand to produce the next slide. Several heads turned to look at us, fists over their grins.

"Actually." Anthony leaned close again when Miller's attention focused on the slide. "I'm pretty sure that's the shadow of doom as the dwindling Valentine's cart passes you by."

I shrugged while girls, and a couple guys, gasped in gooey

awe as they received flowers and cards, balloons and stuffed animals.

Miller sighed as he stepped aside for the frazzled delivery guy. "We may as well address the elephant in the room." The lights came on, spotlighting the cornucopia of leftover love.

The remaining empty-handed women perked like premenstrual poppies eyeing fudge brownies.

Miller brushed the long hair from his face, scanned the insane floral arrangement gifted to one of the most beloved sorority girls. To be facetious, after asking permission, he plucked the card, then read aloud the love note in the most melodramatic manner to make the class laugh.

I couldn't stop chewing my lip as the squeaky wheels rolled past.

No worries, Kins. The day isn't over because you leave campus empty-handed. This jerk has no say in whether you're wanted or not.

My fears subsided when cart boy halted and placed an enormous vase of violet roses before me. I peeked at the girl nearby, ready to slide them to her. He pinned me with a look and flicked the label. *Kinsley Hayes.*

Tears crystallized my vision of another vase crammed with orange calla lilies and white roses. He tapped my name on that envelope like a smart-ass, but I cupped my gasp in girly awe not even Assholio Anthony could steal. Orange calla lilies were my favorite. *Had Daddy taken pity?* The guy dragged a giant bear from the bottom, then a bunch of balloons fastened to the lily vase jostled free and smacked him. Now, I chewed my lip to stifle a grin while he muttered and tossed several cards and a box, then slid a vase over to the girl along with a couple cards.

Holy crap! Look at this stuff!

"Wow, who knew I was such a beloved bitch, yeah?" I

beamed at the jerk-off, but you better believe I was praising God for this wonderful vindication even if I knew I shouldn't.

Miller homed in on his next victim. "I can't speak for everyone else, Ms. Hayes, but I'm dying to see what's inside that wrapping."

The girls leaned in as I took the wrapped present in my hand. The foil paper shined with scrolls of red and silver. He glanced at my fingers as I picked at the edges.

"You save wrapping paper?" he asked, a light in his eyes. I nodded. He reached for a nearby paintbrush, then slid the tip beneath the folds. No damage. "All done."

"Thank you." I avoided looking anywhere else as I held the only jewelry box I'd ever received from someone other than my father. He didn't buy me things that came in flat velveteen boxes. "Wow." I sighed, uncertain how to digest the gift I revealed as I opened the lid.

My teacher whistled amid the coos. The sorority princess jogged over, eager to be in every limelight— one of few girls not intimidated by me. *She* intimidated *me*, though. When she offered to clasp the necklace around my neck, I sputtered a 'yes' and ponied my hair aside.

"This is magnificent, Kinsley."

With deft piano fingers, she adorned my throat with a dainty vine of emeralds and diamonds. She was right: the piece was magnificent, and too generous!

She and her sisters gabbed about pairing the jewels with dresses and shoes. I fought tears, fuzzy and yearning to know what fool spent such money and didn't leave a note.

Mr. Miller cleared his throat while I held mine. "Analogous color palette with your eyes, Ms. Hayes. I'd surmise someone bought that to compliment your irises."

Oh hell. What a deep statement.

I studied the leaves and flowers between my finger and

thumb. No more denial, I wanted butterflies and sentiments, pining and playing, affection and romance, to make others want to gag themselves over my public displays of affection with someone. *Dammit to hell!* This jewelry had the strength to kidnap my resolve as long as I wore this collar for someone's leash! *Get this green Kryptonite off my neck STAT!*

"Coach Walton is going to be nervous if you have a boyfriend."

"It's a good thing I don't," I sang.

"You might after this. Someone in that stack could be the lucky winner."

The sorority sisters speculated like high rollers making wagers with a bookie. Teach winked as I rolled my eyes, then he moved to the next Valentine victim, quoting Shakespeare from her bouquet. *The Sisterhood of the Traveling Pants* followed him to gush elsewhere.

"You were saying?" I cheesed at the sobered face beside me.

"Guess some men enjoy castration."

"Well, let's hope at least one of them has cojones big enough I can't fit my snips around."

He snorted with a reluctant smile while I removed the necklace and reflected that Mr. Miller had summarized every reason for my dedication and why I wanted none of the rumor mill. Being myself was bad enough without adding a relationship or love interest to the drama. Guy beside me: case-in-point.

The warm and fuzzy faded after I replaced the necklace with the care of a surgeon.

The cards were a myriad of corny and adorable, with heart candies strewn on elastic included inside of one from one of the guys Jase had threatened at the bar. *Wow. Guess Jase didn't scare everyone?* I read the verse from the card on the lilies but didn't recognize the handwriting or the source. A pretty poem about never leaving.

Finally, I addressed the arrangement of violet roses—three dozen of them—that I'd tried to ignore like the nag of intuition. As I leaned up to smell the soft purple petals, I spied a card wedged deep between the blooms, *tied to a pumpkin spice Keurig coffee cup!* My heart slammed with hope.

When I ripped the envelope open, Moonlight confirmed with his unmistakable message:

Kinsley,
Not simple or easy, love?
I'll buy that, but you failed to mention you were fast.
Keep those spikes on.
X- Complicated

CHAPTER 10
KINSLEY

When class ended, I was tripping over the balloons to get out and call Tyndall during practice! I needed to run! *Can we say exhilaration overload? Moonlight used my name! He knew my name!*

Miller insisted on helping me to my car because he didn't want me mugged for the necklace. "Excellent point," I agreed, but couldn't kill the dumbest girly grin.

"I've heard your face can freeze like that," he teased.

"That's a good thing, right? Who wants a stick up their butt like the poser from class?" I tried not to rush him as I lost control of my rapid pace. "How do you handle art snobs? I prefer my Han Solo poster much more than that last piece. But if you paint a line and make a million who's the real idiot?"

He chuckled and shook his head as I forced the giant bear into the messy backseat. "It's possible Walton will like this development. Hard to slow you down, Hayes."

"That's good stuff. Make sure you tell him if you see him."

"Sure, but you've been forewarned: he's not happy today. I figure he'll try to take it out on *you*."

"Sounds like you know him well," I said. We teamed to shove all the balloons inside with no success. "Thanks for the advice, Mr. Miller, but I don't think even pissy Walton can bring me down right now."

The pain in my cheeks confirmed how idiotic I must've appeared. When I bent into the front seat to tuck the necklace in my purse, I snagged a pocketknife, then shoved the bag beneath the passenger side. I came up brandishing my weapon of choice with mischief. Miller's smile grew.

"Screw it." Grasping the lot of strings tied to the balloons, I sliced them free, and we watched them sail into the sky with my spirits. "Like blowing out candles on a cake," I sighed. "All those wishes. You should make some, too."

"No way. Can't keep up." When I smiled back at him, his phone was up, and he'd snapped a photo. "You mind? School paper? I assist the journalism department where I can."

"Fair enough. Thanks for your help and the lesson in sophistication today." My smile tamed in shame. "I'm sorry for my petty part in the lecture. I should've ignored Mr. Anthony. I didn't mean to disrupt or disrespect your time."

"Think nothing of it. I was more bothered by him wishing someone injury over their differing perspective. Might be worth reporting?" he suggested. Immediate dread caulked the cracks in my happy moment. I shook my head.

"Maybe if I wasn't so close to graduation? Not worth the flack that might come as a result, but if he becomes a problem, I'll keep the idea in mind. Thank you."

"All right. I won't press." He turned away after a wish of good luck with Walton. "Oh, and happy Valentine's Day, Kinsley."

"You, too, sir!"

I locked the car and headed for the locker room. Ten

minutes later, I had earbuds in. While Coach thought I was running to my warmup music, I gushed into the mic to Tyndall like a dang fool.

"So," Tyndall said, "you're telling me you think the guy who requested *Big Girls Don't Cry* is the workout dude from the beach who is *also* the pirate from the elevator two years ago? If so, this guy sounds suddenly very persistent. How do you know it's him? Did you hear an accent or something? By the way, I love that my brother had to sing that," she snickered. I fought the urge to mention his kiss and sudden flirtation.

"Right?" I giggled then cleared my throat. "Well, there *was* an accent at the bar, but what I recognized at the beach was uh...um...."

"Was what?" she demanded.

"It's hard to put into words."

"BS! You have too many choice words for me when it comes to men in my life. Out with it!"

"His *cologne*," I blurted. "It's so delish, I can't forget it. He wasn't wearing it when he was working out, but when he opened his car door, the breeze picked up, and I smelled it when I was getting into mine. Like it was trapped inside." Heat hit my cheeks even if she couldn't see me. How embarrassing. "Don't make fun or give me crap, unless I call you upset that I was wrong! Please be super happy with me? Tyndall, the asshole pirate is maybe admitting he's ready to man-up, and that he *likes* me despite my being a jerk!"

"Ha! Or he thinks *you've* grown up." *Nice.*

"Kins, this is crazy. Two years is a long time to wait to make a move. A very long time to think about someone. Maybe he was married and got a divorce for you."

"Ugh. Don't say things like that. How awful."

"It's seriously awesome he remembered you after so long,

which means he never forgot you. I'm envious. You know I'm the first to admit that girls get a little dumb and reach for coincidences that mean more than they do, but I'd never fault you for loving his scent. We should pay a visit to the perfume emporium and exhaust ourselves trying to find his cologne so I will know what to buy you for your birthday."

"All right, you...."

"Psh. You'd love it. I bet you'd spray it all over his coat and wrap yourself inside like your favorite blanket."

"Because that's what you'd do?" I shot back and grinned.

"Whatever. You need to hide this from your dad. I mean, remember how bad he flipped his crap when you made out with the guy at the murder mystery dinner last year?"

I cringed at the memory, but my stomach dipped a little in remembrance of the rush.

She continued, "But, seriously, how will you wipe that ridiculous smile from your face if I can *hear it*? You're too obvious!"

"He might buy that I'm thrilled, because I wasn't a troll who received no gifts?"

"Like me?" she asked.

My face fell, and my stride faltered. No wonder she'd made that snide remark about Moonlight divorcing. *Double crap.* Walton picked up on the motion at once. When I went silent for too long, she forced a laugh.

"I'm kidding. Why do the untouchables send you flowers, but the only one you *want* flowers from is too dense or high to realize it's a holiday? And I hate carnations. They remind me of my grandpa's funeral."

"Oh, Tyndall. Please tell me you're not still slaving over the same man-child you told me about last year. I thought we were past him."

Walton jogged up the track to intercept my misbehavior.

As though this were a game of football, I juked and maneuvered around him. *Hell, yeah. Thank you, Daddy!* I told Tyndall he had smoke billowing from his ears. "I have to go, but we're revisiting your relationship issues later. He isn't good for you. You're too great for someone trashy."

"So are you," she retorted. *Gasp!* "Easy, girl. I'm talking about my brother."

"That's mean." *Did she know about the kiss?*

Did they have an argument? No secret Jase was an overprotective asshole who cock-blocked his little sister like his favorite sport. I didn't mind. She was too pretty for a douche who wouldn't put down the drugs and video games long enough to notice her. *Maybe Jase was onto her?*

"Sorry. We're reversed. I hate Valentine's this year, but I love that you don't. Thank you for the chocolate."

"Hey, only the best for you, baby," I mimicked her brother. "And those came from him. Not me."

"Right, because Jase remembers holidays without the help of women. Oh! I have to go, he's beeping in!"

That wasn't Jase she hung up on me for, but the sleaze. Though this sucked, I felt better for my foolishness.

Walton laser-beamed the worst of evil eyes. I sprinted around the bend where the hurdlers practiced, and called for my girl, Eliza, to move as her teammates started. She shifted lanes in time for me to clear the first hurdle. The girls beside me hauled more ass than they typically put forth during practice. When I cleared the tenth and final hurdle in the hundred-meter row, I sped past Walton with his stopwatch. "My time?" I asked with a smug grin. His finger rose, but his lips thinned when he read the clock. Yeah. He didn't have to say. "Didn't even have my spikes on for that one." I cheesed and beat my chest, then did a high kick like a cheerleader.

Walton fumed, but lost his fight with the smile I provoked. "Eliza! Hundred-meter hurdles! *Now!*"

"Thanks, show-off. Now *I* have to suffer," she muttered. "Want to run beside me? I think it'll help my sprint."

"Sure! Same here. Mind if I put my spikes on first, or would you prefer the edge?" I teased. She giggled and shook her head, gesturing up at my face in question.

"Kinsley, you look like you just won the decathlon. You're radiant. What gives?" I had no choice. I told her about the card and flowers. "In that case, get those spikes on, girl!" She beamed excitement and looked around. "Hell, he might be in the risers somewhere!" *Oh no!* My face fell.

"Oh," she hurried, "I didn't mean to scare you. Forget him. Hop to! Walton's gonna get onto you!"

Too late. Walton blew the whistle far longer than necessary. Eliza leapt into action while I hauled to the duffel I'd left in the stands to grab my spikes.

The stuff Tyndall said about my father rang true. If he realized the guy from the 'lift' drifted back into the picture to cloud my eyes with hearts, he'd turn into a worrywart. The only pirate he'd entertain me falling in love with had better be on the Bucs football field scoring us box tickets. His words.

How to hide this happiness? A sneaky call to my dad. He answered on the first ring.

"Happy Valentine's Day, honey. Will you be hungry after practice?" He'd prepared for our annual dinner to make me feel like I didn't need another guy yet.

"Daddy, do me a favor? Take Mom somewhere romantic, just the two of you, instead of our third-wheel norm? I got called into work tonight."

"You sure, Kins? You never work on Valentine's Day."

"Positive." *Negative*, but when I wished them well and hung up with my dad, I called Marcus, so I wasn't a liar. After arguing that we'd made a deal and he wasn't one to go back on his word, I assured him that I'd like to help. He sighed, then sounded like I'd made his whole week. "You short-handed?" I asked.

"Something like that," Marcus told me. "Things need your brand of cheer, Little Red." The background noise drowned his voice.

"Say no more. I'll be there, sir." I hung up and laced my spikes, then pulled the earbuds and tossed them with the phone in the bag.

The whistle piped to such an incessant extent, I worried Walton may pass out. I suspected he had an underlying reason for today's attitude, perhaps the same angst I'd experienced in Miller's lecture and possibly Mr. Anthony's attitude problem, too. Couldn't hurt to blend respect into my sarcasm.

As the zipper traveled the tines on my duffel, I looked to the stands. My breath stuttered as I spied a Bucs cap in the top corner. Same color.

Moonlight? A single red rose rested against the stranger's smile.

One of the track team's managers, my biggest fan, (Looney) Lucy ran behind me to grab water and wave at someone. The Bucs hat waved back, and my heart regained its normal rhythm. *Not Moonlight.*

He was here for her.

"Blocks! Now, Micro Machine! I swear, girl, you're going softer than an infant and a puppy wrapped in Charmin toilet paper!" My heart leapt to my throat at Walton's berating. I caught another smile from the guy in the stands, this time with Lucy nowhere nearby. "Get out here before I mummify your ass with it!"

Jeez. Walton and I exchanged silent anger as I stalked to the blocks.

"Got your number, bud. Now you take mine." I quirked my eyebrows.

"There's the bitch I know and love. Stay away from babies, too. At this rate, you're likely to get knocked-up in the prime of your career."

"Walton! How dare you? Because it's not like *I* have a vested stake!"

He smirked and nodded while I bent and positioned my spikes on the blocks.

"If it weren't for me," I said, "you'd still be doing private sessions instead of assistant coach while ours is on maternity leave. She might decide to take more time with her baby and pass you the job, so man-up and quit being a coward!" I shouted as he jogged down to the hundred-meter finish line. He kept me in suspense on purpose. "Your fear is showing, and that's more contagious than any baby! And since we're on the subject, I'm sure she'd love to hear your opinion of them!"

He blew his whistle. I shot from my spot, determined to make him eat his attitude. When I finished, *he didn't even clock my time!*

"You make an excellent point about cowardice, doctor. And maybe after putting up with you for the better part of four years, I don't want this job. Now get the hell off this track, so I can train your replacement if you screw up. Oh, and happy Valentine's Day." He looked right through my shock and awe. "Overheard the others saying you got some serious merch this year. A fancy necklace? Watch out for guys who buy jewelry. Big price tag, big expectations. Keep em' closed, Micro Machine." *He was serious!* Not an ounce of humor. And he never used my name when he was angry. "*Go home, dammit!*"

"Fine. You want to play that game?" Shoving past him, I trudged to the duffel bag and traded for tennis shoes, then trekked up the hill to the car. I wanted to look at the stands so bad, but my pride refused the pleasure.

Coach meant to scare me off, but he was wrong. While his crass bitterness stung a little, I could see his misery wanted company, but my company was too joyous to keep, even after his rant. And...maybe I could see some paternal fear overshadowing his professionalism. He was like the stepfather I'd never needed. About twelve years younger than my father, but he'd invested a great deal of his time and care to my personal career. In addition to crafting workout regimes and aftercare came the responsibility of what I ate, when and if I could drink, and even the negative effects of dating.

When I had a weakness, Walton bore the burden of building my strength and worked me through the emotional and physical setbacks. He'd never missed a single race, meet or invitational from the day my father had procured his exclusivity during my brief desire to be just like Allyson Felix and take home an Olympic medal. Although I'd changed my mind about going for the gold, even fired him to keep him from wasting his talent on me, he'd applied for an assistant coaching role and scored to keep me in shape. When I tried giving up on him, he'd never let me give up on myself. He'd never left my side.

Now, I was graduating in a few months. A lot going on there for him.

When I strode back onto the track, I hauled that stupid bear and the violet rose bouquet with me. Bayleigh was right. If a woman wanted answers, she had to reach for them on her own. If Moonlight *was* watching from the stands, and one-in-the-same as the pissy pirate, this ought to provoke him.

The girls stopped practicing to come ooh and aww. I'd taken the card out and tossed the sentiment on the passenger seat. When Eliza bent to smell them, I asked her if the guy in the hat was looking our way. "He is," she said. "Hard to tell if he's watching us or not, though. Too much shadow over his face. The rose is tapping his lips." We shared a private smirk while I coaxed stems from the bouquet to hand them out to the team. They were beautiful. I hated giving them away but loved their smiles. When Lucy took hers, she blushed in flattered excitement. I cast careful indifference and turned my attention on Walton, forcing the bear into his open arms.

"Who are those from?" he demanded, awkwardly fumbling with the stuffed animal. "You better be worried if these are from the same guy as the jewelry."

"Walton, I have no idea. That's why I'm okay with spreading the love," I smiled. "My guess is *you've* gone as soft as that bear. You need to take the stuffed animal and give it to whoever she is before she goes home thinking no one wants her, because *you're* too big a wuss to tell her. If total strangers can give gifts like these to someone who scares them, you have no excuse. And I'd like to just accept some happiness rather than worry for now, thank you."

The girls cleared out at his order. Eliza whispered that the man left, but that he'd delivered another surprise. "Come visit me later, yeah?" I asked her. She turned and nodded, then headed to the locker room.

When we were alone, Coach thanked me the way one guy might thank another. No eye-contact. A nod. I slapped a hand on his shoulder and warned him to double check that nothing with my name was in there before he gave the bear to her. "Even add your own card with a handwritten note?"

He sighed. "What if she doesn't like it? Doesn't soft repel girls? Nice guys finish last and all that? Girls like guys who treat them like crap."

I chortled and shook my head but couldn't deny inside myself that Tyndall was a perfect example. "Not true. Never treat a girl like crap. No one would ever accuse *you* of being soft. You're not an all-around nice guy, and since when do *any* of *us* finish last?"

He grinned at nothing in particular. "Touché, Hayes."

"If you promise not to slack up, go for it. I'll promise the same. For the record, Coach, sometimes going soft doesn't mean you're weak. It means you're ready to face the danger. Courage is irresistible."

CHAPTER II
KINSLEY

Wednesdays were country nights at the bar. Valentine's Day served a mixed basket of date night couples and singles crying tears into beers or looking for other lonely hearts to copulate with. Should be interesting to see who'll be picking a bartender's brain tonight. If there wasn't some douche in an Inferno vest, I was all ears and patience.

When my tires crackled over the gravel parking lot, I noticed the employee spots filled to the max, and included Jase's truck after his hiatus to help Rustin move. Neither of us were scheduled. This was a pleasant surprise.

My car fit into a tiny spot. I wished for a sunroof to climb from instead of the skinny shimmy I performed to get out. After readjusting the outfit I picked rather than the skimpy uniform, I reached for the rose bouquet that had rested on top of my duffel after practice.

Eliza better show if she'd watched him put those there!

The bump of bass beating the walls of the bar foretold a fun night ahead.

My boots crunched all the way to the sidewalk at the front,

where Gustav, one of our bouncers, stood guard by the door. He whistled as he took stock. I measured right at his elbow. "Looking cute tonight, Red Running Hood. Are you working?" The low depth of his voice vibrated in my chest.

"Yes, sir, I am. Thank you." I pulled a rose and passed the flower with a wish for a great night.

"Bless your tiny heart. Have fun, Kins. Got y'all covered for the evening."

"Always reassuring when you're on, sir." I grinned over my shoulder and peeked at the row of cars. A bright white Tesla glowed from the best spot in the lot, right beside the bar. I said a giddy silent prayer.

He tugged the door open to the sound of a band of men covering Shania Twain's *Any Man of Mine* and the bar singing every word. Gus and I snickered.

I wasn't over the threshold before a drunk girl draped me in her arms.

"They're wild tonight, girl. Good luck."

"No joke," I muttered and wrapped a supportive arm around Lucy.

Dammit.

Eliza tugged her away with an apology. "Think you're her Valentine, Micro Machine. Catch ya on a free moment when I'm not babysitting?"

I nodded. She pointed at my boobs and mouthed that they were cute. We giggled as I thanked her. My shirt brandished a smiley emoji with hearts for eyes. You can guess where the eyes sat.

"Dunno, I like those shorts and boots, myself," Rustin's drawl hummed near my ear. I turned, and he stole the flowers, passed them to Bayleigh, then captured my waist. His other hand grabbed mine to guide me onto the dance floor in an expert two-step. Bayleigh fanned herself and cracked a fake whip behind his back.

Rustin spun me beneath his arm and pushed the small of my spine in different directions as we got into the groove of the quick music on the chorus. The live band was silly, and I looked up to see Jase doing backup vocals with the country headliner. My head tossed with a cackle. "What the hell?" They both smiled down at us while they harmonized like a couple smart-asses. "If you guys bust out, *Man! I Feel Like a Woman,* I might have to dance with you later!"

Jase's eyebrows quirked in the middle of lyrics.

Rustin hooted and told me I'd just sealed my fate. "That one's been done."

"No freaking way!" I cheesed. "I'm bummed I missed out, and since when does Jase sing any of this?"

"There's much you don't know. Now snap to, girl!" He navigated us between too many dancers and did so with an impressive grace.

"You're kinda good at this, ain'tcha, Country?" My drawl mocked his. After I spun so my back met his chest, I watched our toes to prevent stepping on his.

"Not kinda, Mizz Hayes. Very," he told me over the music. His mouth brushed near my earlobe. "I'm impressed you're able to keep count. Thought I'd have to put your feet on mine to do anything with you."

"Smooth! What's that they say about *assumptions*?" I grinned over my shoulder and took his hand holding my waist to unwrap his grip as I spun away and into the waiting arms of a nearby stranger standing around. Before he denied, I goaded him onto the floor. Rustin's smile brightened. Undaunted. Challenged as I left him open and alone.

"*You*, sir, need another beer!" I craned my neck to peer up at my new partner. Before he flirted or came up with a cheesy line, I took his empty and steered him toward a wallflower watching the crowd and wishing to dance. She perked up, and I slinked behind the bar to clock-in, then grabbed a full tray and let Bayleigh catch me up on drinks and tables. "Did you get a rose, Bay?"

"Only about two dozen from different patrons! Hey, Chad came up here a few minutes ago looking for you. He said Eliza told him you'd come to work tonight." *Hmm*...Chad, my favorite deejay, wasn't on schedule for a couple more weeks. Never pegged him for coming in on a country night, either.

"Did he say what he wanted?"

"Think he needed to ask you something for the paper," she yelled over the juke beginning *Redneck Woman*. The crowd sang along like a choir, and I loved their contagious spirit. "He's around here somewhere. If I see him, I'll point him in your direction—oh! There he is! And there *he* is!" She spun to face me and took my hands from the tray to lean in till our chests touched over the bar. "Give a discreet look to your right when you lift your tray. Chad is talking to Moonlight! I'm giving you a beer for Chad, and you can say one of these chicks bought it for him."

"I'll do you one better. Add a rose, and I'll tell him they're both from me. Gonna pretend not to notice Moonlight unless he says something." We shared a wicked grin. Butterflies practically flew from my mouth.

"Hey, baby." Jase's baritone sounded before I had the chance to lift the tray. I whirred to face him, tingles choking adrenaline straight to my throat.

"Happy Valentine's Day."

"Happy Valentine's Day, Jase." My speech was too breathy, and I swallowed sudden anxiety. "I had no idea you guys were back in town."

"Who's the flower for?" he asked.

I gnawed my lip and hated that I had to tell him since he and Chad didn't talk. "The guy over there from a patron. Bayleigh put it on my tray," I lied, feeling awful for not getting him something. *Why? We'd never exchanged gifts before ....* "Can I get you a drink, Jase? Cool you're helping with country tonight. Didn't realize you knew any. Let alone that you were willing to toss your pride and panties out onto the floor."

Gosh, this was like my freshman year in high school all over again!

His lips crooked into his sexy grin. He put a palm on the bar and stepped closer to cage me. I swallowed and backed against the wood. Another server came and swiped the tray I'd arranged, vexed as she took in Jase's proximity. *Yikes.*

"Who's that flower really for?" he pressed. His eyes smiled, lips straightened.

"Chad," I confessed. "I brought enough for the employees." *Why was I jumpy?* "There's one for you, too, if you want."

"Thought you said you didn't know I'd be back."

"Jase! What's with the interrogation?" He drew close. The heat of his body collided with mine.

"Ready to own up to that dance?"

Um. "Depends." I smiled to disarm him. "You the type who likes to put a choke hold on your partner while you two-step?"

"Nope. I reserve those for the dudes who mistreat chicks." Okay, I now noticed he must be several shots in, goofy, flirtatious. Odd he cornered *me* out of all the women in the bar on such an opportune night. "If I don't manhandle you into a headlock, you want to dance with me?"

"What if I put you in one?" I teased his buzz. His broad smile came out, and his hands wove their way around my waist. I squealed when he lifted me to plant my feet on his. I had no choice but to throw my arms around his neck to keep from falling back.

"Guess I don't mind, but thanks for asking first, sweet Kins."

"Nice." I wanted to ask him questions about why the unusual desire to prove he could dance, but he got to the floor and told me I was leading because he didn't know how to do this. "Seriously? Need the sister to help a brother out?" My smile brightened as I stepped from his feet and instructed him to take proper form.

"No Junior High weaving back and forth?" His lips quirked into that crooked grin before his lower lip popped in a pout.

"Nah, middle school boys are too touchy-feely for their own good."

His fingers dug into my shirt. "That how your ex behaved when you were sweet and innocent?" His eyebrows rose. I almost giggled at how protective he seemed over the kid I used to be.

I shook my head and stepped back, forcing him to follow in a leading way.

"You saying I'm no longer sweet and innocent?"

"That I can't figure out. You seem to be, but leave just enough doubt to keep me guessing."

"Which means you don't pry Tyndall's brain for information," I teased, but inside I cheered because he wondered about me!

"That a dare?" he threatened in big brother mode.

"Really, Jase? I was playing. Can we please not discuss exes? I'd rather forget. I'm in too good a mood, and I'm certain the two of mine are nothing compared to your too many to count." We continued to move, and he didn't once grind on my toes with anything but his mention of my high school ex,

Jack Carter. "Did you get any cool valentines?" I shifted subjects.

"As a gift, or for someone else?" His head tilted.

The jukebox changed, and while the dance floor crowded with canoodling couples, Jase's neck snapped at the song that came on as if someone jabbed a finger in his shoulder. A cover of *All I Wanna Do* by Halestorm. I looked at the music player to see what rattled him. Chad leaned against the wall beside the glowing touch screen with a gutsy grin but shrugged and gestured over his shoulder like another had picked the music.

"That guy...." Jase trailed in irritation. "Confessing his intention, eh?"

I scoffed at the absurdity. "Now I know you've had too much to drink. He's a deejay. It's Valentines. He may not be on the clock, but knows how to get people on the floor. However, I am on the clock, and I'm going back to work."

"You mad at me? Sounds like you're saying I don't know how to get people on the dance floor."

I gazed up at him with a soft smile, my hands on his chest. "Don't put words in my mouth. Take a flower and quit being big brother. Have fun." After a placating kiss to his cheek, I turned and strode up to the bar, asking Bayleigh to hand me another rose for Jase and an update.

"Everything okay over there? I can tell you were catching crap. Guess what that means?" Bayleigh grinned.

"When he thinks Chad is coming onto me? Yeah. Big brother mode, Bayleigh. Enough said."

"Right. I'll play blind, but can we adopt a seeing-eye dog?"

CHAPTER 12
KLIVE

"Afternoon, Mr. King."

"Good afternoon." I greeted one of the parents at the Children's Cancer Center. He rushed to hold the door while I juggled flowers and bags into the lobby.

"You're gonna make the rest of us look bad," he joked.

I chuckled and shook my head. "On the contrary, you're a warrior. I'm just an awed bystander trying to help your fight."

"I appreciate that. Are you volunteering today?"

"If they'll let me," I told him.

"Well, I know Evan will be glad to see you," he said of his son.

"Ditto. Tell him I'll be in after a bit."

He nodded and meandered down the hallway.

"Oh, Klive, how sweet of you to think of this place today. Don't you have someone special you should be with instead?" Nurse Lynn rushed from her place behind the reception desk to remove several shopping bags from my hands.

"Only you ladies." I grinned.

"That's too bad." She smiled before peeking inside a bag

109

filled with rainbow acrylics. "I'm assuming these are for today's art therapy class?"

"They are, and these are for all of you." I set a large vase on the desk beside colorful fliers and schedules.

"Thank you!" Lynn gushed. "They're beautiful!"

"Indeed. Tie-dyed daisies are perfect inspiration for today's class," the art therapist said as she joined us. "Maybe we should bring these into the art room as a visual aid?"

"That's a great idea, Greta," Lynn told her. "He came bearing supplies, too."

Greta thanked me and took the vase while Lynn carried bags into the hallway. I headed back to the car to grab stacks of old newspapers, but threw two new ones on top, then hauled them inside to the art room. Multiple bald heads and bright sets of eyes turned my way. Several siblings and parents dotted the chairs beside their loved ones and held paint brushes in anticipation.

"Klive! I'm happy to see you!" Ten-year-old Hannah clapped her hands and waved me to sit beside her and her mother, Adeline.

"Give me a moment to pass these out, then I'll come over, all right?"

She nodded.

"Here, don't want you taking all this weight on your own," sixteen-year-old Evan said as he walked up. His eyes smiled above dark crescents. I shook my head as he tried to remove half of the stack from my arms.

"You're a good man, Evan, but the only one I'll let you help me with is the one on top. I happened to circle and highlight some points of interest," I told him with a wicked lift of my eyebrows, grin to match. His expression shifted to an adventurous glee as his teenage interest piqued. After double-checking to see if his father heard us, he gently raised a paper from the top while his dad was in conversation.

I sauntered over to Hannah and asked her to take the other one from the top and read the front page.

"Okay," she said. When she collected the paper, she noticed the ones beneath were different.

"Trust me. Just read. Let me know what you think when I come back."

The art therapist greeted her class, then placed a speaker on the counter behind herself. She told everyone to visit while she prepared. Instrumental harp thrummed a calm and contented vibe into the room before she dug into the bags of supplies I'd brought. Cabinet doors opened and closed as she rummaged for items and stowed others.

The kids and parents nattered about life as only they experienced the unpredictable days and weeks. Two other volunteers passed out cups of water and paper plates. I paused at each station and spread newspapers beneath the tables and below canvases on small easels, spoke with each family while I went.

Only one soul here today knew life without the sting of cancer. A first-year medical school intern. She busied opening tubes of acrylic paint and dotted paper plates with the color palette.

I'd never had cancer, but my little brother, August, fought for two hard years before winning when he was fourteen. Our lives took on such a different meaning that we existed like aliens who visited the Earth of shallow problems and humans every time we finished a hospital stay or chemo treatment. As a result, I feared hospitals, but faced my fears when donating marrow and finding a match at the Cancer Center. A child. Hannah. My first mission to save a life rather than taking one. Atonement.

I knelt near Evan and spread papers beneath his area. He folded the newspaper I'd given him. "King, do I want to know why I'm reading about a gifted university track star in her final season? Is this supposed to inspire me since I'm in my final stages of chemo, because the only thing you've done is caused new pain if you feel me? The one you circled is hot. Her teammates are too."

"Where's your dad?" I asked from my hands and knees.

"Getting wet wipes from the teacher," he said.

"The girl I circled is the one from the elevator. Bitchy Bonny," I said so only he heard. "Kinsley Hayes."

His jaw dropped as he slapped the page with her photo. "No way. *The* Anne Bonny from your Gasparilla story? She looks too wholesome to dress the way you told me. Even in that uniform and letter jacket."

"Ha! You haven't seen her at work." I fished my phone from my jeans and showed him a photo I'd taken while Kinsley leaned over the bar. Her shorts climbed high on her thighs; calves checked from standing on the tips of her toes.

A dumb grin mingled into the shock in his face. "You have to bring her to visit."

"Who?" Evan's father asked. I yanked the phone under the table and shoved the device back in my pocket. Evan cleared his throat as I stood up and placed paper beneath his canvas. "Oh, I know this girl." Evan's father pointed at the paper. "The one that's circled. Kinsley Hayes. She goes to the same church as my wife's sister."

The medical intern squeezed in next to Evan and dotted paint onto his paper plate. "Ah, Micro Machine. Her cousin is in the medical program here in town. I've never met her, but everyone's afraid of her except him. He swears she's nice, but you know how legends grow. Apparently, her drive caused her last track coach to go into premature labor three times before she quit her job and gave it to the personal trainer Kinsley hired for the Olympics. They say she was vying for a spot on the US team but chickened out because she's never lost a race and is too afraid to lose."

I laughed before I noticed her lack of humor.

"Don't believe me? Go to a meet and see her temper for yourself. But don't let me steal the moral from the story of the article. That writer knows the rumors as well as we all do, and he's always on the lookout for something to redeem her character with. Supposedly, she's gearing up to fight the diabetic crisis one child at a time as a nutrition counselor. Admirable, considering she's not taking the typical Kinesiology route that athletes on scholarships usually do, but I hope she has a better manner with children than she does toward her peers on the track."

I couldn't assess whether this girl feared or admired 'Micro Machine'. Perhaps a mixture of both with a large dash of ignorance.

"Why not talk to her?" Evan asked her. "You know, see for yourself if the rumors are true?"

His dad gave a more-or-less nod of agreement and we all looked at her. She shrugged. "I don't know. I'm just a lowly undergrad who can't even jog for thirty seconds without coughing up a lung. She's about to graduate with an advanced degree and an athletic ability that makes the papers. What would I say?"

The girl moved onto the next table and seemed to move on from the subject of Kinsley just the same. Evan's dad shook his head in wisdom and said, "What a shame. Never know what you *won't* know."

Evan grinned at his dad and told him he made no sense, then he looked at me. "I think legends are the stuff that drives explorers to the ends of the Earth in search of the truth in them. Ya know? I've faced down chemo and death. I'd talk to this girl in a heartbeat. She doesn't scare me."

"Atta boy, mate. You got yourself the makings of a brave man," I told Evan's father. Evan grinned in knowing. I left them in order to continue laying my paper trail until finally settling on a stool beside Hannah.

Spinning her paintbrush, she made a whirlpool in her water cup while awaiting instructions from the art therapist. "Here, Klive," she said. "You can share Mama's canvas."

Adeline and I smiled at one another and shook our heads. "You know," Hannah's mom whispered, "she's just nervous we won't see you anymore when she triumphs over this disease." A mite of doubt clouded the smile of certainty in her words. Adeline was nervous she wouldn't see her daughter much longer if this disease won the war.

I glanced at the art therapist as she apologized to the class for the delay. Only a few more minutes, she promised, she forgot something in her car. Out of the room she dashed, and I took that moment, due to the fear in Adeline's eyes, to pull a tiny velvet box from my pocket.

"Oh, Klive, no. I wasn't implying—"

"Shhh, Adeline. It's not what you think, dear. You both know one woman has my heart, and today I came to show her to you."

"Is that an engagement ring, Klive?" Hannah asked in excitement. I urged her with my hand to lower her voice, double-checking to be sure no one overheard and created a new rumor. The others were too busy talking amongst themselves, thank God.

"This, Hannah, is something I had made just for you as you enter the last leg of this race against cancer." They both gasped as Hannah opened the box. A white gold bumble bee perched atop a dainty white gold band. "Do you know that because of the weight of a bee's body, science itself says it shouldn't be able to fly?"

She allowed me to place the ring on her middle finger, the thickest of her bony digits.

"Is that true, Klive?" she whispered in awe as she stared at her gift.

"Would I lie?"

They both granted big smiles and shook their heads. I continued. "Do you know why it flies?"

"Nuh, uh. Why?"

"Because no one told the bee that it couldn't fly, the bee flies anyway. Now, look at me and listen close." I held both of her tiny hands in mine. Her skin was cold. She leaned in like we shared a secret. "No matter what you believe to be impossible, it *can* be possible if you believe. When you feel weak, feel yourself second-guessing the pain of the fight, your endurance, you look at this and let it remind you of the truth. All things are possible with faith. Do you understand, Hannah?"

She nodded. Her whole face brightened. "Is that why you also gave me the story about the runner? How she's so short she shouldn't be able to run so fast, but she keeps winning anyway?"

I sat up and marveled at how she noticed what I hadn't. "Fantastic observation." In the picture featured in the paper, Kinsley stood with her relay team. They each smiled in their uniforms and college letterman jackets with medals around their necks, but Kinsley was at least half-a-foot shorter than the second shortest woman in the bunch.

Picture in hand, I pointed at the star of the article and said, "May I introduce you both to Calico Jack's Anne Bonny?"

"Shut up!" Hannah squealed and threw her arms around my neck the way a grown woman might've after being gifted a ring in a velvet box. But she thrilled for having a face to her favorite character now. How many times had she asked me to retell her the story of how I'd fallen for the meanest, prettiest girl at the pirate festival even before I'd gotten there? An edited for children version, of course.

"Oh, Klive, have you talked to her? Did you get her a present for Valentine's Day? Why are you here with us when you should be on a date with her? Oh, my gosh! Oh, my gosh! Oh, my gosh!" She plunked down on her stool and clapped her hands. I'd never seen her brown eyes shine with such radiance. *What a feeling!*

The therapist rushed back into the room and introduced her Valentine husband to the group. She held a huge vase of red roses and wore the most wonderful smile comparable to the love glowing on Hannah's face. The class awed. Adeline leaned closer to look at the article and the ring on her daughter's finger.

"Thank you, Klive. That ring is perfect. We couldn't be more excited for you, right Hannah?"

Hannah sighed with the most romantic look up at the ceiling, and I chuckled. "Oh, you hopeless females. Whatever shall I do with you?"

"Bring her by to meet us?" Hannah rushed. Her mother nodded and agreed.

The art therapist asked for everyone's attention. Adeline handed me a spare paintbrush. We each dipped into the blue for the background and touched our bristles to her canvas. While Hannah followed directions, I said low for Adeline's ears only, "I haven't yet spoken to Kinsley. I sent her two sets of roses then watched her give them all away."

"Why on Earth would she do that? Does she know they're from you? Or that you even exist?"

Adeline speckled shades of blue while I dappled bits of white clouds to hers and Hannah's canvases.

"I believe she gave the roses to others who hadn't received any gifts, because I noticed she gave away a bear I didn't buy her. She knows who I am, just not by name because I'm playing secret-admirer games with her. I get the impression she's not the type you fawn over, and she comes running. Considering the venom with which she told me off during our first encounter, I don't quite know what to expect."

"If the rumors I overheard are true, and what we've gathered from your story and reading, confidence goes a long way. To strong women, heck most women, nothing is a bigger turn-off than insecurity, Klive. You're the least insecure person I've ever met. Your confidence alone instills it in others and makes us all question why we ever had a doubt about a good outcome. It's one of the reasons we love when you visit or participate. I don't see how she couldn't use someone to continue that confidence as her life is changing. Just be yourself."

"Changing? What do you mean?"

"The article said this girl is graduating. I haven't gone to college, but I remember being scared about graduating high school for what comes next. If I were her, I'd be worried about my plans for the future coming into the present, especially when she leaves that running career behind. Oh, crap, they've moved onto their flower and we are still painting hearts in the sky. Here, hurry before she sees!"

Adeline grinned and rushed to rinse our brushes before we attacked the stem and leaves while the therapist made her rounds to our side of the room. When her vibrant face looked into mine, I relished the true friendship in her expression, rather than unrequited love. I'd never confide this weakness for Kinsley to anyone else.

"Hey, Klive, do you think Mrs. Greta would be upset if I

added a bee to my flower when we're done?" Hannah asked all aglow.

"Well, Hannah, you can ask me yourself, but I think that'd be a great idea. What gave you the inspiration?" Greta asked, her hands behind her back as she appreciated our work. Greta's eyes smiled as she ruffled my hair and praised Hannah's ring. "Yes, I believe the whole class could benefit from adding a bee to their daisies, and after class is over, Klive, you may hand out your daisies to each of them. This way they don't wilt on our desk."

Later, after the last flowers were handed out, Hannah and Adeline hugged me goodbye. They each took the remaining two daisies.

Adeline asked how I felt.

"Quite content. Why do you ask?"

"Because Kinsley gave all her flowers to others. Now, you see why you shouldn't take it personally. Happy Valentine's Day."

Good point.

"Happy Valentine's, ladies. See you soon. Text me when Hannah's next treatment is scheduled, and I'll come visit."

"Will do. Goodnight!" they called out to the art therapist and her husband.

The room emptied. Only the sound of instrumental harp chimed through the air. I helped stuff the speckled newspapers into trash bags while Mrs. Greta and her husband washed paintbrushes. Her husband gathered the filled garbage bags and headed to the dumpster outside.

"We go to church with her family," Greta said over her shoulder. "She's not as scary as the kids at school make her out to be. She works the nursery with her cousin and babysits for us when we want to go on dates. I'd say she's better with children than with her peers because children haven't yet learned the cruelty of the generation she's cursed to be part of. Think about it. They'd rather have everything handed to them on a platter, so they don't have to work. They judge anyone who works for what they have as being given something they've never had. That's why I love this job. These kids and their parents live for what matters."

"I couldn't agree more."

"Kinsley is dedicated at a level her peers can't understand because they come to Florida to party at the beach between classes. A pity she didn't become a doctor. Always nice when you get the physician who graduated with ropes and honors rather than the C student. I don't know your beliefs, but you're welcome to attend church with us anytime if you'd like a proper introduction." She focused on stubborn red paint stuck to the neck of a brush to avoid the response she guessed was coming.

"I'll consider it," I said, rather than outright refusing. She needn't know that God and I weren't exactly kosher.

"Klive, you don't have to stay. I'll help her with the rest." Greta's husband returned and kissed her on the temple. His arms folded around her waist. "I can think of no better date on Valentine's than serving alongside my beautiful bride," he said against her temple.

She giggled and turned her face to his for a kiss. I rushed outside to gulp the humid breeze. I didn't want to think about God or the impossibility of the situation. I'd rather pretend that with Kinsley my own advice would prevail, that all things *were* possible.

The parking lot held only three cars: Greta's parked beside her husband's and mine alone on the opposite end. I felt like my car, isolated, while Jase parked nice and close to the girl I wanted parked beside me.

CHAPTER 13
KINSLEY

"Is this for me, Kins?"

"To you, from me, yes, sir-ee. Don't let your ego read too much into it," I teased Chad. The rose rested on the bar between us.

Most couples were on the dance floor and hanging out at tables. This afforded me a small lull to chat. He sat on a barstool opposite, enduring the country songs, claiming they'd be better with his special twist.

"I think they sound great." I shrugged.

"Oh?" He pinned me with skeptical amusement and an accent straight from Down Under. "And your bias has no bearing whatsoever." He peered at Jase and regarded him with similar suspicion as Jase did him.

"The roses? Any idea who sent them?"

"Roses?"

"Yeah, the ones you received during Miller's Color Theory lecture. Lucy couldn't wait to tell everyone how you showed up at the track with them." I rolled my eyes and sensed Lucy's boring into me this moment. "If Micro Machine has someone special cheering her on during her final season, it's more for fans to cheer about. Everyone loves a happy ending."

"Good grief. Chad, I have no idea. Secret admirer." My lip sucked between my teeth in debate. *Should I ask him who Moonlight was?* He'd flip for even a mention of the 'Complicated' story I held to.

"Secret admirer...sounds intriguing." He grinned like a guy who saw I held my cards close. "Playing. I won't write about it unless you confirm."

"I appreciate that. The song? Someone else, or were you trying to drive Jase up the wall?" I tested, my poker face in place.

Chad chuckled, pleased I asked, but we both knew there was something unsaid hanging in this game. "Both. He's tipsy. So protective of you. Easy equation. Did *he* give you a gift, by chance?" Nice. He wasn't giving me anything on Moonlight unless I gave him something.

"Hmm...I suppose it's possible the roses might've come from Jase, but no. Nothing I know of."

Chad nodded in contemplation. His fingers twirled the red stir stick in his drink. He looked out at the stage and the crazy crowd.

"Before you ask—no—the blond didn't get me anything, either, but seriously drunk patrons gave me a bunch of corny gifts and inappropriate invitations." We both laughed, but I found intrigue in how hard he searched for a significant other to write into the picture of my life. *Why the sudden interest?*

"All right, I'll let it go for now. I only came to drop your article. Figured it might be positive publicity for you and this place. I noticed police reports released for this location about Inferno incidents. That's not you guys' fault. Hope it helps." He tapped a stack of papers he'd placed at the corner against the wall beside where he sat.

"That's nice of you, Chad. Even if it *is* weird having a spread on my career. You're making me soft. How will I remain tough to get the job done?"

Chad scoffed while I slid a pair of Blue Hawaiians across for a couple a few stools down.

"I know you too well, *Kinsley*." I loved the sound of my name with his accent. He knew and screwed with me all the time. "You've got that down whether or not you're soft for a split-second. Hope you like the feature, darl. I'll see you around campus. Take caution with Inferno." I nodded and let him kiss my cheek. He snickered as I leaned away to look at him. "Taylor is frustrated. Have fun with that. Fill me in when he takes you off the market that way I can really piss in his Cheerios."

"Chad! Shame, sir. Behave."

"Never." He stood from his stool. "Happy Valentine's, Micro Machine." He handed me the rose I'd gifted him. "From me, to you." The bud tapped my nose before I snatched the stem from his naughty hand. I shook my head. Bayleigh tsked with disapproval as she wound behind the bar to grab a full tray.

"I can't wait until this day is done!" She shouted over her shoulder. Chad's attention diverted. "If I get one more stupid, grammar school Valentine or box of chocolates, I'll need a bigger uniform!" Her joke was hollow. She seemed bothered even as she tried to sell her humor. Chad waved her off, disappointed she didn't have something more interesting.

After his departure, the tension in the staff became more obvious as time wore on, and I was no exception after a few hours. My smile was real, but I made orders like a machine. I lost myself in contemplation over the things Chad had said. *Police reports for this address about Inferno. As in—there had been more than I'd realized. How come no one mentioned anything? Why hadn't Marcus put together a meeting or told us whether Sara was absent, or had officially quit?*

In another bout of generosity, I stayed through closing, hoping someone might gossip when the crowds deserted, but no such luck. Everyone was tired and serious. The fun vanished from the bar. Usually during clean-ups, we'd put the jukebox on free play and dance with our brooms and mops, trade lyrics during sing-alongs, choreograph the rare routine to pull customers.

Not tonight.

Jase gave an excuse to stay, but made Rustin go when the country band finished packing. Even he seemed sobered and somber. The quieter everyone became, the louder I wanted to shatter their silence with a scream. *Did they all know what the hell was going on and refuse to tell me? What purpose could that serve?*

The hallway was empty, the locker room clear, the dishes done, and the glasses rehung. The floor mopped, tills counted, tips divvied, and everyone filed out. Jase walked to my side and grasped my hand with an expression that asked permission. My smile tired, I took what he offered. The night was still except for crickets chirping as we trekked outside. When we got to my car, Jase stilled me with his hand at my cheek. I memorized the callouses and texture of his fingers. His eyes held emotion, *exhaustion or more?*

"I missed being around you, Kinsley."

Oh!

My breath hitched, and my cheeks plumped with the stretch of my lips. "What a wonderful thing to say, Jase. Thank you. For what it's worth, work is lacking when you aren't on the schedule." No way I could be as forthcoming as he'd been without my face catching fire. Thank God for the darkness. He looked at the gravel for a second, but his grin reflected mine. How flattering to make him look this happy.

"Will I see you at the course, or, you know," he cleared his throat, "outside of work?"

My smile tamed, and I bit my lip. There was a weird vulnerability between us. Like when you're growing boobs, and the boy who saw you as another best friend, sees you differently. I swallowed and nodded. "We'll see."

"That's good. My workouts haven't had the same punch these past few days."

"Ah, you need a woman to run you off the course, eh?" When I beamed up at him, he looked away and his Adam's apple bobbed. *What was happening? Should I stop this?*

"Something like that." His hand left my cheek and traveled to the nape of my neck. My head tilted back. "You're a little maddening, Kinsley." When I gasped, he leaned in and our lips met. Thick fog stole my rationality, and goosebumps broke out over my skin. No way in hell could I stop this. His warm mouth was soft, patient, sweet, slow...*ooh*. My body burned to lean against him and increase this drag.

When he broke away before I felt ready, his lips quirked. "Sorry I didn't get you anything. Figured something homemade would do the trick there."

My laughter filled the surrounding emptiness, ours were the only two vehicles left in the lot. My hand found his arm. "If it was from the heart, that's what matters," I teased, but reeled at the enormity of our axis shifting.

He cleared his throat again and shook his head. My face fell.

"Believe me, Kins, it'd be a lot easier if it wasn't." For the second time tonight, my breath was stolen. "And if all I wanted to do was make love to you, I'd fulfill my lust somewhere else to keep you intact. In case you gave any credence to Chad's song when we were dancing. Not that I wouldn't give my right nut to make love to you, just, damn, could you shut me up?"

Whoa! My smile erupted while I covered his mouth and tried to harness my elation before my heart jumped off my face into his hands. He smiled against my fingers and cupped them with his, then dipped them down and licked my palm like he was French kissing. I cackled and wrestled against him till he released me, then I caught his face and smeared my wet palm over his cheek. He chuckled and snatched my hand then placed a sweet kiss to the back.

"Happy Valentine's Day, baby."

"Happy Valentine's Day, Jase."

He stayed until I got into my car then watched me drive away. Holy crap. *That just happened.*

CHAPTER 14
KINSLEY

That night, sleep was more like a nap. Snooze wasn't a choice since I slept through the alarm. My rigid schedule shattered as I joined the land of the living at five-fifty. In the haze that followed, I tripped twice while wrestling into a pair of shorts and a sports bra, pulling my sweatshirt on backward by mistake.

"Gah!"

The drive to the beach was as foggy as my brain. I forgot my water, and the protein bar ended up being fruit chalk! *I couldn't effin win!* Like a dog with peanut butter, my mouth was sticky and parched, and my tongue kept traveling over my unbrushed teeth to remove that filmy feeling.

Once I parked, the soupy morning and humidity made the sweatshirt a misery. I shucked the fleece, cursing myself for not grabbing a workout tank. Call me a prude, but I felt over-exposed and inappropriate, much the way I did at every track meet—that uniform being as sparse as the work uniforms would be once spring break hit. From then through Labor Day, tourist season packed the bars, beaches, and restaurants.

So much to be pissy about!

Ironic, considering how crazy awesome yesterday had been. Gifts from a secret admirer *and* Jase Taylor kissing me goodnight on the same day? Guilt ate away at my happiness for loving the attention of two men and having no idea which I wanted more. I'd never been in a triangular predicament before.

Who knew Jase had feelings?

What would Tyndall say?

I tipped my head back, and my neck popped. Yeah, the tension was everywhere. The key chain coiled up my arm, and sunglasses guarded eyes heavy with yesterday's eyeliner and mascara against the burning sensation of the rising sun.

My stretch cut in half when a jogger halted his run too abruptly, and knelt to tie his shoe, checking me out the way a thief spies the perfect car stereo to pawn. A knot formed in my belly as he untied the shoe before retying the laces. His gear seemed too new, especially his shoes. The white laces and swooshes on the sides glowed fresh and unused, like the white of his t-shirt. No sweat ring around his neck. I'd never seen him here before, but maybe this was his normal time of day, or his first time gaining the courage to jog in public? But he didn't match his clothing. They didn't fit his vibe and came off as more like a costume.

I chewed my cheek trying to plan my options. *Should I jog my usual route, or go the same way as him? Which one would help me seem less like a scared animal he might want to chase? Maybe I was thinking too much of nothing!*

"Good morning," I offered. Taking in my surroundings, I cast him a dismissive, but polite, smile. He barely nodded as his eyes ate at my body like the starving homeless. I might've dismissed my fear if he could tear his gaze away from my exposed flesh, but I'd come up against a look like that before. At least this guy was alone.

My throat dried in remembrance of the Gasparilla festival two years ago. Two jerks had openly trapped me between them in the chaos of drunken throngs. The groups of costumed festivalgoers had been so thick no one noticed or heard my pleas for the men to get their hands off me.

I cupped my arms at the memory of how one forced my arms to my sides while his fraternity brother tried putting his hands down my corset. I'd screamed and shouted for Nate, knowing he'd never allow them the liberty. Nathan had beaten the shit out of them once for trying to force me into their room at the last frat party I'd ever attended. The brothers took their revenge in the open with the threat that I go ahead and tell and see what happens to my reputation. With all my might, I'd kicked the tip of my boot into the shin of the guy holding me.

When he'd let go, I'd ducked and backed my elbow as forcefully as I could into the other guy's ribs, then took off running as fast as my sprint in high-heeled boots could carry me to my father's building. Their vows of vengeance had assaulted my ears in the mayhem. I remembered looking over my shoulder expecting them on my shadow, praying to reach my daddy's office before they could catch me again. They couldn't hurt me if my daddy was there.

I'd run into a knife-wielding pirate instead.

I released a shaky breath at the memory of his presence, the fearsome command to tell him who'd hurt me. A look like his conveyed action over threats. I'd cried the whole drive home, swiping tears from my eyes with the sleeve of his pirate coat. The first man aside from my father I'd ever—

Nope.

Hush, Kinsley Brain!

The pirate wasn't here. Neither was Daddy, but I wasn't in heels or a stupid costume restricting my breathing or movements, either.

Here and now, I scanned my surroundings. The obstacle course was my best option for safety in numbers. Jase, Rustin, or even beach guy might show up to work out. *Who was I kidding? Beach guy was Moonlight. Moonlight is Beach Guy and my pirate.* Thinking of the way the pirate had put the fear of God into me when he'd held that knife, I was ready to run behind him and point this creep out to him. I wished I had that knife on me now. Maybe I should take the Bowie from beneath my mattress and keep the blade in the car for things like this.

God, please don't let this creep do something to me!

The guy stood up, pulled his phone and pretended to be busy enough to figure out which direction I might go. Or, so I guessed. If I returned to my car and left, he'd see what I drove and my plate numbers. I sighed and stalked to the water fountain, a passive eye on him the way he eyed me, like a standoff. *What the hell?*

The course would fill sooner than the beach. Against my athletic judgment, without a warm-up, I turned and trotted through the tires with cold muscles. My breath rasped harder than normal, a sweat broke over my skin that had nothing to do with exertion, and I kept resisting the urge to peek over my shoulder. By the time I jumped down from the block wall, the man turned to walk the way he'd come. I landed with the grace of tossed bricks. He peered over his shoulder, still hesitant. I jogged again to the tires, conceding for my safety.

First work? Now my favorite workout spot? Was nothing sacred?

My right triceps locked tight when I climbed the rope. Fun times trying to slink down without dropping or shredding my palms to ribbons. As a result, I skipped the pull-up bar, and aimed for the net, resigned to jump the wall and go home. The treadmill was a better option today. This time when I jumped, my ankle twisted on impact and my bottom met with the sand in a flash of white pain.

"*Ohhh shit!*" I cried, the injury only part of why tears rushed to my eyes. I pushed my foot out to inspect any swelling. Strained weeping followed with visions of my career flushing down the toilet before the season had barely begun.

"*Whoa!* Heads up!" I had no hope of scrambling away. Someone landed with a curse while I shifted away as best I could. "Kinsley? What the *hell* happened?" Jase demanded, rushing over, bending with concern.

"My ankle." I whimpered, desperate for this not to be real.

"We need to move you. You're lucky I took the one side. Rustin will be over the wa—"

Jase dove over me like a protective shield. Rustin landed against him in an impact I deserved. Jase cursed. Rustin cursed *at* him, demanding to know what the hell kind of moron— "Red?" he cut off. "What are you doing like this?" He shoved Jase's arm out of his way. The first time I'd seen anything but flirtation on his face. "Man, Jase. Now I'm sorry for the foot up your ass."

Jase shifted to squat beside me, shaking his head at Rustin. "She's twisted her damn ankle. Make sure no one else comes over that wall before I can move her. We need ice," Jase told him. "Here, put your arms around my neck, baby." With a nod, I did what he said and let him lift me.

"It's all clear," Rustin called as Jase walked us to safety. "Where will we find ice at this time of morning? The businesses are closed for another few hours." Rustin studied the quiet boardwalk, but Jase trudged toward the frigid waves, the fog stealing the sun's shine upon them. Jase's head looked in Rustin's direction. "Good idea. That water is still cold. You want me to remove her shoes?"

"No." Jase placed his chin against my head. "I'm sorry, baby. This will hurt, but you're used to the occasional ice bath against sports injuries, right?"

"Doesn't mean I *like* them!" I almost howled when we went in. Jase barely flinched as the freezing water swallowed his calves. He was smart enough to recognize my attitude wasn't toward him but resulted from fear and pain. "Oh, gosh!" He dropped to his knees. My legs and bottom submerged all at once. I sucked my teeth and gripped the hell out of his neck, squeezed into his warm body out of desperation.

Mascara melted into the crook of his throat as my tears stippled black droplets to his skin. My body burned for different reasons than last night.

"Shhh...." he soothed. "A few days of rest, and you'll heal. I can drive you to school if you want to visit the sports medicine doctor?"

Rustin waded in, wincing and cursing, making me giggle while I cried against Jase's stubbled Adam's apple. Jase's chuckle joined mine, and Rustin's hand went to the foot I hadn't hurt. He lifted the drenched shoe from the ocean. As my sock rained water, he said, "See, it's barely even got anything wrong."

"Wrong foot, Country."

"I knew that." With a scoff, he gave me his smile, the only visible sunshine on this dreary beach. My injured ankle rose in his hands. The dripping sock carved patterns into the swollen grayish pink flesh. He averted his attention toward the shoreline to avoid my eyes. "You've got some concerned spectators."

My gaze shot over Jase's shoulder. *The beach guy!* Moonlight stood at the water's edge with three others looking on with worry. Part of me thrilled over his concern. Part of me was ashamed, considering whose arms held me.

The reasonable part won out, seeing the attention as a negative. "I need to get out of here with no one knowing I'm hurt. Chad put that article out. I can't afford speculation I might not be able to perform. People love negative publicity, and too many would love to spread some on me."

My tone was rough, angry, frustrated. Rustin nodded like I had a great point. Jase studied my expression.

"Jase, forgive me. I need my daddy. My coach will freak, and I don't want him to unless it's real. My dad can take me to the doctor, then I'll deal with the result."

Jase nodded, cleared his throat and asked Rustin for a favor.

"Yeah? What's up?" Rustin asked, his hands on his superhero hips, his shorts wet up to his thighs. They shared a look. Rustin walked up and reached beneath me. My arms transferred around his neck, and for the second time today, I was uncomfortably close to too much exposed skin that even water this cold couldn't steal the heat from. There was something in how Rustin was a stranger that made this more inappropriate. He fought the waves to get us to the shore, and I looked over my shoulder to see Jase dive below the surf. When I winced in sympathy, Rustin chuckled. "Lifeguard. Remember?"

"Ah. Well, crap. Hope it doesn't look like I needed rescuing," I cracked. My ankle was numb, but my pulse thrummed in the swollen tissue.

"Ha, I think *he* needs rescued, Mizz Hayes." I didn't lean into Rustin's chest or neck the way I had Jase's. I didn't want the onlookers getting the wrong impression.

"She all right?" Moonlight asked him with the faintest hint of an accent, the concerned citizens waited for an answer.

"Yeah, things got a little too hot between them, if you know what I mean." Rustin flashed him a grin. My jaw dropped, and my hand snapped against his chest. Moonlight shook his head and looked at me from behind sunglasses.

"You all right?" he demanded, scary and soothing at the same time.

Like that night in the stairwell. I found my voice.

"I'm all right, thank you for asking." He gave a tight smile and a curt nod. The others I vaguely recognized from morning routines also nodded and went about their business.

I tried to quit studying him. My mind homed in on the pain in my ankle, focused on every panging nerve rather than looking like an ungrateful slut in the arms of another.

"Rustin, will you please set me down? I think I should try walking."

"No ma'am. Not until we get to the picnic table, Mizz Hayes. Want me to toss you around a little to make it seem like I'm not overcompensating for your injury?" Before his offer registered, he shifted me in his arms and tossed me up and caught me like a child while I squealed in laughing surprise against my will for all the butterflies set loose. He tossed me again while I giggled breathlessly and shouted that he put me down.

"Fine. Have it your way." He set me on the picnic table. While I caught my breath, I provided my car key and instructed him to get the phone from my console. In the meantime, Moonlight did rounds on the course. His sunglasses seemed to aim in my direction multiple curious times. Dark hair matted with sweat the harder he pushed himself. He was doing pull-ups when Jase walked up with a kiss for my cheek. Jase took to the course like he wanted me to watch him instead. The pain bloomed thick with my embarrassment at getting caught and passively called out.

Rustin, breathing a little hard, slapped the phone in my empty palm with a triumphant ray of sunshine printed over his mouth. Wagging that tail .... "Thanks, Rustin. Excellent job, boy, now go play." I teased him, then dialed.

My father answered on the first ring. "Daddy? Have you left for work yet?"

CHAPTER 15
KLIVE

A man I recognized stalked across the sand like a bloke on a mission to retrieve his little girl positioned between two shirtless men.

What caused Kinsley's injury?

Her agility had given my own a great run, yet the bee was at risk of no longer flying. *Nonsense!*

I moved about the course as her father knelt for her to hop on his back. She smiled like a happy girl. Too good at that facade. When I jogged from behind the wall to the tires, he helped Kinsley into the passenger seat of a BMW. I took that moment to walk over and shake Jase Taylor's hand.

"I hope your girlfriend is all right."

"Girlfriend? Now there's a foreign word with a ring to it." He grinned and thanked me. "I hope she'll be fine, too. If I have time, I might go check on her later." Envy was hard to conceal. "Something tells me she won't be serving my drinks tonight, though." He looked to his friend, and his face was grim.

"Mind if I come watch you perform?" I asked. "Afterward, perhaps we might discuss the happenings at the bar?"

He gave a knowing look, then introduced me to his friend, Rustin Keane. We shook hands.

"Pleased to meet you. Wish under better circumstances," I offered.

While assessing me from behind shades, he returned the sentiment then agreed the recent events at the bar were, "Escalating and unavoidable."

Taylor rested his elbows against the picnic table, his legs open as he squinted against the dull light of day.

"Yeah, I'll see ya later, King."

I didn't expect to see them until the evening, nor did I, but I did see Kinsley.

The end of lunch break had me dashing onto the lift to head up to my office, attire expensive, hair sculpted, impatience showing. About twelve floors glowed on the panel of buttons. I added mine, then weaseled into a corner for spare inches, desperate to keep space between myself and a notorious loudmouth who thrived on passively insulting co-workers in ways difficult to prove beyond hearsay.

Before the doors closed, Kinsley and her father joined the crowded box. The others barely noticed due to their phones. A cold rush gripped my ability to breathe while her father checked whether his floor was lit, then shifted her toward the back. He glanced knowingly at the man nearby and cast me an apologetic smile when he tucked Kinsley inside my personal space in order to place himself between her and the pariah. For the first time, the invasion of my bubble did not bother me. I wished I were free to pull her closer, to hold her as I had that fateful night of Gasparilla. *Oh, to make this crowd disappear!*

Breathe in...two, three...out...two, three....

I almost closed my eyes to recall with vivid clarity how the curves of her hips felt beneath my fingers.

"Daddy, you don't need to do this," she whispered. "I don't even need to wear this stupid thing." His arm secured her waist, she had a splint on her ankle, and she argued that she could stand by herself. The doors shut. Without bumping me or her father, she wrapped her hands around the bar at our backs. *Oh, memories.* At least she didn't want to rip the metal from the wall to beat me over the head this time.

"Mom can pick me up, then I can drive," she insisted. "The doctor said the swelling will go down soon. He even cleared me for work."

"What does that doctor know?" he said under his breath. "He's younger than you are."

"He is not. This splint is nothing more than a melodramatic placebo. Useless and attention-grabbing."

"Kinsley Fallon, there's no use arguing, young lady. Don't make me pull this elevator over."

She snickered while her father fought a grin, then cleared his throat. "I'm taking the day. I'll make calls from my desk at home. This way I can keep you off your feet, and *you will not* work. What happens when someone bumps you or steps on you and turns this into a full-blown injury?"

Excellent point.

I reached for my personal phone to text Marcus.

> Give Kinsley the rest of the week off

When I brushed her by mistake, her head turned in apology, where she did a double take. Her chest inflated. *No way she recognized me in this capacity, right?* But she exhaled in a manner I mimicked, blood rushing to her cheeks and pounding in my ribs. What madness being this close and playing indifferent, especially since her father picked up on her shift and eyed me in speculation.

"Forgive me," I rushed and refocused on my device, determined to throw him for both our sakes.

> 🐨 I can't spare her rn!

> She's injured her ankle and needs to rest

> If she doesn't you could be out a bartender for weeks

> Pick your poison mate! 🍸

When I finished, half the elevator had emptied—meaning we weren't sardines, only a school of fish. Kinsley's father busied himself talking shop with someone I gathered to be a colleague. Kinsley stepped inches away, apologizing and looking down at her foot while she forced the splint to go with her. She didn't glance up, but she spoke.

"Your cologne smells very nice, sir."

A full smile stole from my indifferent sham. My hands traveled to my pockets as I studied the veins in the marble floor so her father— and everyone else— might not notice my elation.

"Thank you. You're the runner from the feature, yes?" My voice was quiet and drowned under the conversation around us, but she nodded without any hearing issues. "I hope your foot is okay." I gestured.

With a tap to her Mona Lisa lips to silence me, she nodded once more. Her hand dropped to her side next to my own.

"I'll be at my meet without an issue." The Mona Lisa transformed into Rembrandt brilliance, then shifted right back. "Looks worse than it is, because my daddy won't quit coddling me."

She had me. I smiled at the wall to stifle a laugh. Her father hadn't heard a word, but we dwindled by more than half of our school. Further communication had to be covert.

What a delicious thrill! What did she think of me without my costume? She was much shorter in flip flops than she'd been in her boots.

A woman in a pantsuit lowered the phone she'd buried her head in and breathed a sigh of relief as the pariah stepped off. When the doors closed, she said, "Oh thank heavens he's gone. He makes me uncomfortable." Several agreed with her.

She looked at the mirrored ceiling in praise, then gasped at the reflection. "Oh, Kinsley, your foot. Andy, what happened to her?"

Amazing what people missed due to social media.

Kinsley sighed as the woman faced her father. I brushed my fingers against the back of Kinsley's hand. Electric shock. Her breathing changed. A muscle jumped in her neck while I clenched my jaw. We had something thick. If this ride didn't end soon, we'd be exposed.

"She's okay," her father supplied, like he knew his daughter was having trouble talking for the moment. "She was running cold on that obstacle course at the beach because some pervert almost accosted her. She had the fortitude not to go to her car so he wouldn't know what she drove, but still."

I inhaled my anger so deep, I had no choice but to add something. "That's unacceptable." I met the eyes and expressions studying our proximity. Kinsley's cheeks flushed while I worried. My instinct to protect her showed too obvious, but hell if I knew how to erase the anger the way she masked her emotion.

"I agree. Absolutely unacceptable," Kinsley's father stated.

They shared a look before the woman picked back up. "What's this world coming to when a woman can't even go jogging in a safe area?"

"I keep telling her to carry a can of wasp spray with her," her father said. "Hose them down from a distance. Get 'em in the eyes. It's not a weapon, court shouldn't be an issue."

Nice!

"Easy to jog with. Nothing odd there," Kinsley injected. She snickered along with the others, the sound thawing in the warmth of her timbre.

"Did you report him to the authorities?" I asked. "Or at least carry pepper spray?" I couldn't resist the dig.

She choked on her giggle and swallowed before shaking her head. Her eyes big, round and guilty, if not shocked I'd spoken directly to her before these people.

Her father studied us then focused on her like a man frustrated and wanting the same thing.

"No. I didn't think of it, and I don't remember him well enough," she told me. A lie. She was lying to my face in fear while I grew agitated. *Had my words in this very building two years ago meant nothing to her?*

"That's a shame. Should you remember, get a sketch and a report this. If you expose roaches, they run. Though your father's bug spray idea is brilliant. Way further reach than pepper spray."

We chuckled together as I attempted to erase the tension.

"See?" Her father nodded.

"Yes, sir. Thank you," Kinsley said.

My anger vanished at the stung look on her face. *Dammit. I didn't want to embarrass her!* I wanted to squeeze her hand and tell her I'd squeeze the trigger of my gun if this happened again. Things were becoming dangerous at the bar with

Inferno, now the beach. I had more than enough suspicion to merit a tail without being a stalker. *I should have gone to the beach sooner, dammit! I might have caught that wanker red-handed and dealt with him then and there! Was Inferno responsible for this? What the hell was their angle?*

The lift opened on their floor, and her father bid the rest of us adieu. He aided his beautiful daughter through the doors. Her limp resulted from some bastard making her scared and trying to steal my bee's wings. *This was not okay!* Hannah was looking to Kinsley as a source of proof in doing what you shouldn't be able to. Two powerful reasons to fight for one person's safety, activating my powers of evil for good.

Kinsley peered over her shoulder with that bloody silent plea that wrapped my fealty and fury around her tiny finger.

Anything you want, love.

Could she read my answer?

The doors closed. I avoided the dancing eyes studying our magnetism. Pantsuit lady was sure to gab to her entire break room at the earliest opportunity.

When I got to my office, I locked the door and grabbed my other phone to call the only man I trusted for this job.

"Christophe, I need Joey for an exclusive amount of time," I told my private investigator.

"Concerning?" He multi-tasked in the background.

"A protective detail."

"He's on yours."

"Not mine. A woman's."

"A woman?" He stopped everything. The background noise muted. "Who will watch *your* back? I'm too busy managing the rest of my staff, and Joe is the only one who knows your double trouble." *Double life.*

"I suspect this pertains to the double trouble. Not a direct threat, but one great enough I need an extra set of eyes protecting this girl. I want to hunt without distractions. May I have him, or not?" I struggled with my exasperation. The stack of messages on my desk proved there were many things to take care of before I went to the bar, if I got the chance, and I didn't need to add more to the list.

"I'll move him at once. What's the name? And you never answered my question about *your* back, King."

"Eric can watch mine. Her name is Kinsley Fallon Hayes. She's mid-to-high profile." I referenced the article and some of her background, then told him about the bar and this morning.

"Klive, is your interest professional or something more? Be honest."

I didn't want to hear shit about how dangerous a romantic attachment was. I knew every instance with her could equal a target on my head if I couldn't recruit a replacement in time.

"Professional. One of my bartenders quit this week. I won't lose another because some prick can't keep his hands or knob to himself."

He whistled. "Professional. Right. Joey's texting now. He'll be on point in about an hour. You have a phone number to trace?"

"Not without going through personnel files at the bar. Have Joey text Marcus. He's got it."

I hung up, my jaw clenching, palm tingling to do permanent damage. Something larger was afoot. *My* bar. *My* staff. *My* girl. *Who could know that, though?*

If only I could ask Kinsley what this asshole looked like. Before I went off the deep end, I had to admit some degenerate could have targeted her at random. She revealed more skin than usual this morning, but that shouldn't matter. Damn near every female jogger in the Bay area revealed more skin than necessary, and that was their prerogative and shouldn't mean writing an invitation to some tosser.

My fist pumped a stress ball before flinging the foam across the office. *In...two, three...out...two, three....*

Thirty minutes later, I received a text from Joey.

Target acquired

Bitchy Bonny back on the radar 🔥 😎

I rolled my eyes.

CHAPTER 16

KINSLEY

Moonlight is here! 🤍

Sexy huh?

Bayleigh texted during the shift *I* should have been working.

> Bayleigh Blue! Get to work n quit creepy stalking. Marcus will notice 😎

If stalker wasn't in the job descrip how would we memorize peep's drinks? Tonight's drink of choice, Captn n Coke w cherries and grenadine 🍒

> Wish I was there 😿

Me too. So do they. Get well. XOXOXXX 😿 😿

Missing one of Jase's performance nights was as weird as the developing relationship between us. I giggled. Above her caption, she'd sent a picture taken near the stage. Jase sat on a stool with his guitar and the mic in front of him. Rustin perched beyond. But, in the left corner, at the coveted table, sat a man wearing a black fedora with a red ribbon.

I sighed and scrolled back to his photo, zoomed in on the back of Moonlight's head. If I were bolder, I'd beg her for a face pic. He was so...sexy, sophisticated, handsome ....

"All right, girly. What's got you smiling that way? That's not just any sigh." My father sat on the porch swing beside me. My feet rested on his lap. He had removed the splint to alternate massage with cold compresses. The tissue was tender, but nothing I couldn't have walked through. Still, I'd spent my day doing school work from my laptop on the couch in his study and trying not to daydream over the intriguing reunion I'd had with my pirate, not to mention how scary attractive he was in business mode. No fear of ticking me off in front of my father, either, that one.

Daddy's intuition had been fired up ever since, and he'd disappear only to reappear with a snack or soup like I was sick, then peek at my notes or my screen expecting doodles of hearts with a boy's name or something. Poor guy.

"It's Bayleigh texting me from work," I told him. "The music's good tonight." I showed him the picture.

"Ah. Mike's boy." *As in Michael Taylor.* "I noticed Jase on the beach with you this morning...."

"Ha! That's because it's hard *not* to notice Jase on the beach, Daddy." I gestured at his physique since Jase and my father had comparable builds, my father was a mite smaller and less defined in his late forties, but I earned a laugh out of him the same.

"True. Is that normal?" *Oh, boy.*

"Meh. We have similar workout regimens. Nature is preferable to the gym, yeah?"

"Yeah." He nodded and rubbed while I tried not to wince at the residual pain. "All right, I have to know. Are you dating?"

"Daddy, how in the world did you get that idea? You know I'm waiting until after I graduate. Jase and I are friends."

His laughing outburst nearly knocked me off the swing. I clawed at the wooden armrest like a cat falling from a tree and gaped as though he were crazy.

"For real, I'm *not* dating."

"What about the guy from the elevator?"

"What?" I gasped. Heat warmed my cheeks. "The pirate? What about him?"

"Pirate?" He leaned back to study me. All humor vanished. "I meant today. The man you stood next to. You looked at him like you recognized him. *He* seemed uncharacteristically coy beside you, not to mention candid and protective once he learned what happened. Is *he* the pirate you told me you met in the elevator?"

"Uncharacteristically? As in, you know him?" I danced away from the question.

"Why? Are you pushing for more information? Because for the right price, I may have what you're looking for."

"Daddy! Stop. No, I don't want his information, (*liar!*) and I have never seen him before. He was...scentastically pleasing and *uncharacteristically* handsome, sir. I mean, cut me some slack. I'm still a woman, even if I'm behaved. If I got the caveman going in a man like that one, wouldn't be the worst thing in the world, eh?"

He stopped rubbing my ankle and put his face in his hands.

My nose shriveled. "That's gross. Who knows where my feet have been?"

"Scentastically?" he laughed. "It's a good thing you earned

that scholarship, because the words that come from your mouth...." He trailed off and grabbed my feet again but didn't rub. "I love you, Kins. You're too pretty for your own good, and that's not my biased opinion. The whole office was talking about it in the break room after reading the paper. Everyone's praying for you to nail your season. I downplayed your injury."

"Thanks, Daddy, but that's because there's barely an injury to downplay, but that's sweet of them on all accounts." I chewed my lip for a moment. "Today was scary. Thank you for coming."

He grew angry in a snap. "The man in the elevator was right. We need to report what happened to you, and maybe it's better that Jase was around. You should time your workouts so he's there. Not trying to—"

"Whoa. Slow your roll, Pops." I set my phone on my belly and lifted my hands. "I didn't mean the weirdo from this morning. I'm not going to report him, because it could've been my imagination going crazy, but better safe than sorry. I meant my career disappearing in an instant. It got me thinking about things I've been ignoring."

"What do you mean, honey?" I winced when he traded the warmth of his bear paws for the cold compress.

"I mean, I've been working hard at being the best and staying that way, but what happens when it's over? Not like I haven't known this time would expire, but what comes next? What do I have to show for myself aside from a room full of medals and good grades? Is work and scholastic achievement everything?"

"Oh, boy," he sighed, deep and aging, weary of holding a facade. "Kins, do you remember when you were little, and we'd go to the park?"

"Yeah, Dad." I grinned, being a smart-ass. We could see the playground from our front yard. Old-fashioned streetlamps illuminated the empty swings, merry-go-round, and seesaw. Most of the kids who'd moved into the neighborhood when we were all little were teens or grown. Now, the main use of the slide was a make-out spot. On occasion, neighbors gathered to grill on one of the barbecue pits or play soccer or football in the undeveloped area. "Do we need to go swing over there?" I teased.

"When you're able to hobble over," he cracked like a smarty.

"Nice."

"Anyway. When we bought this place, you were only five years old. I couldn't wait to get you on the swings and the seesaw, but you had no interest in the equipment. You loved making me chase you through the oaks. You'd reach up and try to touch the hanging moss, even if you were twelve feet shy." We chuckled. "As much fun as I had, I wasn't sure I'd catch you in time if you tripped over one of the roots on the ground. At first, that's all I had to fear. Then, you discovered the open field. That grass hadn't yet finished growing. Divots and dips everywhere. It didn't matter. Once you got your feet under you, you were a quick little thing even back then."

"What happened? Scraped knees?" I grinned. "A tantrum?"

He smiled as he looked at me and shook his head. "No. I was that good." He winked. "You were the best practice for keeping me in shape."

"You're such a humble man, Dad."

"Thanks, your mother tells me the same thing all the time."

She walked out, then arched an eyebrow at our position. Dad and I pursed our smiles. I pulled my legs off his lap to let her sit there. After asking how I felt, she handed me a cup of decaf.

"Am I intruding on anything important?" she asked.

"Of course not, Claire. We love when you join us."

She snorted but snuggled up to him and ran her maternal expression over my face.

"Daddy is getting all sentimental on me and talking about the playground. Me running away from him. Think he's afraid I will do that now that I'm growing up?" She and I shared a laugh while he shook his head with a wry grin.

"Young lady, that wasn't what I was getting at."

"Pray tell, Andrew, let's get down to it," my mother said. Her fingers wended through his hair like he needed soothed. "It's late, and your *grown-up* daughter is a night owl, but *you* are an early bird who has to be back at work tomorrow, mister. No more days off before vacation. You don't want to upset your boss."

"Yes, ma'am." He sighed and gave me a pointed look. I cringed. "As I was saying: the real danger wasn't in the obvious roots and things. You ran right over them. It was when you discovered the open field. You'd take off like lightning, throw your arms out and stare up at the sky like a bird about to take flight."

What was the point of this story?

He read the confusion on my face. "The running wasn't the problem. It was that you'd close your eyes and run, enjoying the mystery in where your tiny legs might take you. I'd have to predict your steps to keep you from tripping or running into the street. The harder I had to work to keep you safe, the harder you giggled. Like it was all a dangerous game."

"Daddy—"

"No, Kins, honey, hear me out. You're about to graduate. I can tell today startled you. Men are coming from the woodwork like they knew you wouldn't date until you had your degree. There's a field coming. You're about to be in the open, and this time, I can't predict your steps. If you trip, it won't be fair of me to save you. Lord knows your mom is right.

You don't even think of yourself as an adult, and you're in your mid-twenties."

"Daddy...." I swallowed hard, unsure what to make of how serious he was, or how my mother stared at the chains on the swing instead of me. At my father's prodding, she stood up. He did, too. "If you guys want me to move out, you can just tell me."

"No, honey. Don't miss the point."

"What's the point?"

"Kinsley Fallon Hayes, don't play dumb with your father."

I sighed and looked at my toes instead of them. Lonely feet with no more lap to lay on.

Daddy kissed the top of my head and wished me a goodnight. I gave him a pleading look.

"I'm sorry for whatever I've done. I love you. I don't want to upset you, and I'm not dating. Honest."

"But you will be, and it's okay. I'm not upset. You've done nothing wrong. And you're not the only one here who has to grow up and move forward, baby." He grasped my mother's hand, and her eyes softened, no longer avoided mine. "Just do me a favor, Kinsley Fallon?" he asked.

"Anything." I nodded, a lump in my throat.

"When you want to throw your arms out and fly, don't close your eyes."

CHAPTER 17

KINSLEY

Between Marcus banning me from the bar until Monday, and coach ordering me to stay home until the same, I was going stir crazy. By Sunday morning, I needed out. When my daddy saw me come into their house for church wearing heels, he threatened to march me back up to my garage apartment to make me wear flats.

"Dad! My ankle is fine!" I all but pouted. I didn't care about the heels. I was making a point.

"No, ma'am."

"Yes, sir," I countered, my eyes determined. "It's this or working out. I'm not sitting around and getting fat on all your sick food."

"My food is not sick," he argued in mock offense. I couldn't hold my anger with him, and he knew that. "You love me. Be a good girl. I'd be more comfortable with you doing a *light* workout than walking in high heels."

"Deal."

"Uh, uh. A light workout. Promise me."

"I promise! What do I need to do? Spit in my hand before we shake?"

He chuckled and ruffled my hair before we shook hands. I marched outside and up the stairs, into my place for those flats and another run of the hairbrush. At church, I felt like a Hobbit for how short I was compared to everyone around me. My dad liked the contrast. Jase's dad did, too.

"She's miniature without high heels!" Mike Taylor gushed and threw a brawny arm across my shoulders. Jase's tiny mother, Bianca, stood the same beneath his other. He and my father joked about our statures and made small talk after the service finished. My mom gabbed with all her girly tea party friends and discussed plans for their next frilly event. Itching to get out of there, I was practically pulling on my dad's sleeve, urging he take me home.

"You doing the potty dance, little bit?" Mike teased. My dad grinned and filled him in. Mr. Taylor nodded in understanding. "Jase is at the beach. You should stop by his stand and say hi after your workout."

"Already?" I asked in surprise.

"Yeah. He's helping with lifeguard training and prelims."

"I might do that, you know, after I get the ants outta my pants."

"Guess I'd better end her torture, Mike. It's always good seeing you. Perhaps your son will join on a Sunday soon?"

"Always working on that one. He's stubborn. Think a reminder that sweet Kins attends might be in order?" Mike asked. "Jase tells me you got flowers on Valentine's Day."

"Did she?" Daddy asked. My eyes closed. *Dammit.* I'd given most of them away and assumed my father had gotten me the calla lilies since the card they came with seemed a passive way of begging me to never leave.

"Hey, how did Jase know?" My forehead creased in

confusion. He'd only seen me with the red roses, and I recalled telling him I'd brought those for the employees.

Mike dipped close like we shared a secret audible to everyone. "Young lady, if there's one truth you can always count on no matter how old you get, it's that your parents will hang you out to dry when grandkids might be on the horizon."

My jaw dropped, and Mike's play morphed to triumph. Daddy's riotous laughter drew attention as he tipped my mouth shut. My mother's hands clapped and cupped to her chest.

"Did I hear something about grandkids?"

Ugh. Now, I was crazy ready to get the hell out of there! At this rate, the church gossips would have caught the tail-end of that conversation and been fast at work spreading a pre-marital pregnancy that didn't exist with a man who hadn't attended in years!

Daddy ended my humiliation after they shared a few more jokes. Mike and Bianca kissed my cheeks, then pumped me up about their daughter's plans to visit during spring break. "Hey, I'm playing," Mike said. "But if you married Jase, I'd have the perfect sister for Tyndall." His elbow tickled my ribs. Jeez. Gloves off.

"Yeah, no pressure there," I teased with a dry tone.

Minutes later, I scooched into the back seat of my dad's Beemer. "Come on, Daddy! Before you guys plan my wedding! My proverbial tie is too tight, I tell ya!"

"Our evil plans worked!" He cheered. Mom slapped his arm as she grinned over her shoulder.

"You'd make pretty babies with that one," Mom said.

"Are you crazy? Could you make it more obvious you want me to end up with Mike's son? It's like I'm in junior high, only in junior high Jase was the boy you'd have warned me about.

Suddenly, it's okay to have his children?" I crossed my arms over my chest. "This is an alternate universe."

"Welcome to the wonderful world of what you call 'adulting'."

"I don't use that word."

"Well, little rebel, now you know who got you flowers on Valentine's Day," my dad offered.

"Psh! For all I know, Jase has no clue he got me those flowers because you and Mr. Taylor hatched a plan to make him look good the way I did with Tyndall's box of chocolates. I mean, how else did he know my favorite flower, Daddy?" My eyebrow arched as he glanced in his rearview mirror. Mom chuckled to herself and looked out the window. *That woman...* I had my answer. Had she sent that necklace? I asked, and my dad almost stopped the car in *OH HELL NO!* panic.

Mom's hands rose in surrender. "Easy! All right, I confess! It bought the necklace! She's too tomboyish. I just wanted her to look like a lady."

When we got out at the house, she shot me an expression that said she'd saved my ass but had *not* sent jewelry. I played along. We watched dad go inside to make lunch, and her nails skimmed my arm.

"May I see it?" she asked. Her green eyes searched mine in seriousness. I nodded and so did she. We went into my apartment. She dug through my fridge for coffee creamer while I grabbed the velveteen box from the bedroom. When she turned, the box rested on the island. She looked at the velveteen like she needed a newspaper to kill a gigantic roach. I'd not seen that look since I'd sprained my ankle in ballet.

"Kinsley Fallon...." She opened the box, a reverent gasp following. "This *wasn't* Jase. It's not a crush purchase." Her French manicure ran over the diamonds and emeralds. "Someone's either interested in your heart, your purity, or the combination. Someone rich. This is not cubic zirconia. You be careful, Kinsley."

"I will, Mama."

She evaluated my expression for a few beats before yanking me into her arms and kissing my head. "Oh, my baby. Here I am telling you to grow up, talking about babies, and I...I...I'm not ready. My baby. I know you hate this. Just let me hold you for a minute without any sarcastic comments. Just be still and know how I love you."

"Mama."

"Nope. You hush."

I hushed and let her hold me for three solid silent minutes. She released me, stole my creamer and closed the door behind her before I could argue. Alone, I looked down and traced the necklace the way she had. Mom hadn't looked confident that I could handle who might come out of hiding. *Had Moonlight bought this? Why not leave a note like he had for the roses?*

Rather than let the unease expand, I snapped the box shut and hid the treasure once more in the back of my closet, then changed from this stupid dress back into my skin.

CHAPTER 18
KINSLEY

At the beach, I chopped my jog by more than half as I dodged increasing towels and umbrellas once church services let out.

Shirtless men dotted the obstacle course while ladies out to trap the sun's rays hovered like flies as they gawked at the chiseled physiques. A woman sporting an Iron Man tattoo worked out in her swimsuit like an audition for a body-building bikini contest. I joined their ranks while my tank and shorts appeared reserved as sun-worshipers all around shed their layers to absorb the heat.

Even if I'd babied myself and my limits, I'd made fantastic progress. When, at last I finished my core work, I flipped from the girly pull-up bar, and ran an arm across my forehead to keep sweat from dripping into my eyes. My torso drenched proof-positive with victory. I'd kicked my twisted ankle's ass, and triumph over that fear of failure carried an endorphin high that couldn't end yet.

I thought about what Mike said about Jase and the lifeguards. Jase conducted training like the drill sergeant in charge, and I'd skirted past him undetected on the way in. That meant that to get to the car, I would have to pass back by. Now I dreaded the jog, not because my ankle hurt, but because the eye candy in red swimsuits obeying every order from the man who had to watch their every bouncy flounce. Maybe that's why he liked being a lifeguard?

Ugh. Let the torment of relationships and crushes begin. *I hated this junk!*

When I happened upon his realm, the lifeguards took a group break. Jase leaned against the ramp of a stand, his tan darker than most of today's beachgoers. Aviator style sunglasses rested on his nose, whistle nestled between his glistening pecs, his free hand clutched his hip above red swim trunks.

Rustin, the ever-present sidekick, chattered beside him with one of the *Baywatch* bunnies. Jase laughed at something she said.

Go time.

Should I jog in front of the stand, or behind it like I'd done when I'd come in? Translation: was I a wuss, or did I have the balls to say hi?

Abruptly, my ugly bun felt like my hair gave ugly a new name. I tugged the elastic holding my hair and let the sloppy waves flow. Now, he'd have no choice but to notice me.

"Hey, Jase." I grinned with a small wave and kept jogging like I was doing my routine. His chin turned my direction in a way that gave me flurries.

"Oh, no you don't, baby!" he laughed and piped his whistle as if there were a life in danger. My steps faltered. I screamed when he captured me and vaulted me over his head without warning.

"Jase!" I squealed. He didn't put me down and shifted like he would do presses. "You freaking show off! Me Tarzan, You Jane much?"

"No, that's a different position, sweet Kins." He smiled wicked as hell, the innuendo screaming louder than I had. "You all better?"

"I'll be better when you put me down!" I shouted, unnerved by heights and precarious balancing on the palms of someone's hands!

"Oh, yeah?" He teased, then pumped his biceps. I flew up before he captured me in his arms. I pushed away from his hold, but he molded me against his heated skin. "Want to do real-world scenarios?" He looked back at the trainees. I gasped and fought him while he cracked up. When I took stock of our position, we were about ankle deep in the surf and continuing. "Hey, Matt, will you grab her shoes as a matter of safety? Watch her right ankle."

"Jase Taylor!"

"Kinsley Hayes!" He kept going, and this was nothing like when he was icing me down with my swelling ankle. Jase's body-double jogged over and took a swipe at my shoes before dodging my kicks.

"My ankle is fine, and I have no desire to go swimming, sir. You and your twin better turn your bottoms around and remove me from this water right now." I unfolded my arms from his neck to cross them over my chest. Jase and this guy, Matt, chuckled together like I was joking.

"Or else?" Jase asked.

"No more kisses for you." I gave a smug lift of my chin. Matt winced in play pain for his fellow man.

Jase was undaunted. "Is that so? Hmm...last chance. Shoes on or off, baby?"

My jaw dropped. I tugged my sunglasses away.

"You're not serious. You won't throw me in, will you?" My eyes widened from the horror. He shook his head, but not in denial, he seemed affected. *Score! Welcome to my world, bud!*

He continued walking, and I jerked as the fangs of chilly ocean bit into my bottom, soaking my shorts like spreading venom, the pain following. My grip tightened as I tried to pull myself up.

He tsked. "Sweet Kins, seems I got you wet. Guess there's no turning back now." One of his eyebrows lifted with a devious grin, then *he threw me into the dang water!* Pins and needles didn't have jack on this.

Sputtering in shock, I surged free and dove for him. "Jase Taylor! I cannot believe you did that to *sweet* Kins!" Hoisting myself up to his shoulders to push his head down, he went without a fight. The water was painfully cold. His skin had been hot, but he didn't seem to care since he came up smiling when shoving the droplets from his face. One wicked glance in my direction had me fighting the current for safety, but Jase dove and caught me, bringing me back under, pulling us both up together.

"You can run from me on land, but you cannot escape here. This is *my* element, baby," he boasted with a splash.

"You are *such* a player. I'm not falling for this. It takes a lot more than that, mister." I splashed him back, then dove underwater, swimming through his parted legs, rising behind him.

He turned and scooped me up. "I have no idea what you're talking about." Charm oozed from the most adorable look of innocence, making me laugh at the mere absurdity. Tension ensued when he dropped his play. Pressing me against his chest once more, he brought his face close enough to kiss me, but held his position. Great. The breath caught in my throat like he was about to follow through like Valentine's Day! The tantalizing memory of the last kiss he gave me floated like a ghost between us. *Could I handle another?*

"Oh, c'mon. It's working a little."

With superhuman strength, I grabbed his chin to shake his head no. "Afraid not, sir. I'm immune to your charm." *Psh! May I shake the hand of the woman who was?* One glance over my shoulder showed there were a few pissy women still on the beach suffering from an addiction to his charm, and they wanted their fix. *Not too keen on sharing, huh, ladies?*

"You mean I'll need to use my superpowers *in public*?" Jase asked. "Kinsley Hayes, this is a big deal. I only whip those out for crime fighting, baby, but you're criminal when you're plastered this way...."

Cheesy idiot.

His smile vanished, replaced by sudden gravity. When this time he descended, low and slow, I gasped expecting another kiss. What I got was an anything but innocent Eskimo kiss, his nose running up, then dragging back down to tickle the tip of my nose. My eyes closed to the thrum of an escalating heartbeat when his forehead rested against mine, his deep inhalation indicative of a desire to take this much further. Millimeters separated our lips and warm heat emanated from both our mouths.

What was going on when the king of easy lays was taking a pointed interest in me?

"Let's restrict those for crime fighting from now on." My voice wasn't as strong as I willed. Whatever his intentions, we were both affected. I was glad for the pain of the chilly water. I'd bet he was, too.

He cleared his throat. "Yeah, I only pull them out in emergencies. Keep that in mind for next time, ya hear?"

I'd have asked how many emergencies he'd used that move in, but before I had the chance, he threw me back into the surf.

CHAPTER 19
KINSLEY

Monday wouldn't come fast enough! The dichotomy of anticipation and trepidation for seeing Jase sing at work, not to mention being hot on my toes once more, had formed knots I couldn't untie. Spring break season—all of March—didn't kick off until the end of the week, but the first Alternative night was always crazy packed. Everyone had the itch for fun. They brought their chaos to the bar and lined my pockets while rocking out with the songs Jase's band, Rock-N-Awe, performed.

The beach was on pause since Coach allowed one workout only, and that workout was under his supervision. He wasn't a jerk, I wasn't a bitch. We didn't fight. I hated to admit that maybe there was something to Coach Walton's incessant lectures about getting enough rest. When I zipped the duffel on my spikes, Walton and I shared our relief, though I knew he fought a silent war on whether to allow me to run. I wasn't saying a word. My sprint was healthy, like nothing had happened.

But so much had happened.

With Jase.

Angst hadn't been an issue until the drive home to get ready for work became a mental rehearsal of scenes with unpredictable endings. Who the hell knew how to play this game I avoided? Most girls, I supposed. Like the type of girl who gave a crap, I used every tool in my arsenal for transforming a hoydenish athlete into a bar-maiden babe.

An hour later, I tied the tiny lap apron over the black shorts and admired the bonus of training in the sun. Five-foot-two never looked so long, lean, and cut when the sun kissed all the right places. *Whoop, whoop!*

My father turned into the driveway. Well, hell. To delay until he went inside, I double-checked the pearly whites, applied texturizer to tousle the layers in my hair, added more eye makeup than normal, and spritzed perfume in extra places. When I peeked out the window, I growled. He and my mom sat on the swing, which meant he'd had a long one.

Dammit.

I scanned the land mines of laundry—*I should have done that when I was in relaxation mode*—and jerked okay smelling track pants up my legs to cover the shorts. That called for more heaven in a bottle to cover the hell I'd have taken if he'd seen me dressed in this.

Earbuds. Yes. Good plan. I picked a rock song I hoped Jase would play tonight and pretended to be running late as I locked my door and jogged downstairs to my car, tossing a wave with a kiss to my parents. When I was out of sight and on my way, I sighed in relief.

The parking lot up front was half-full and filling quickly when I drove in. There was one spot in our employee area. I snagged the space. Seeing Jase's truck sent adrenaline bursting through the tips of the fingers I drummed on my steering wheel. The clock on my dash read four. Thirty minutes before go-time.

I pulled the vanity mirror on the visor and took a tone with my reflection. "You can do this. It's Jase. Tyndall's brother. He's only a guy. Get your cowardly ass out of the car and get to steppin'."

I exhaled as I opened the back door. Jase's voice carried over sound checks, joking with patrons as the band set up. The locker area was empty but gave me extra space to remove my pants and put on my game face.

When I sauntered out to the floor, the band goofed a cover of *Don't Fear the Reaper* while they asked for certain mics to be turned up, drums down, etcetera. I tucked myself behind the bar to help dry glasses, and Bayleigh hung them up since she could reach without a stool.

Her eyes bulged when I failed to stop singing when the band stopped playing.

"Crap!"

"No wonder you don't come on karaoke nights!" Bayleigh stooped down to have a laugh attack, egged on by a patron shouting for "More cowbell!"

I slapped my forehead and felt the heat light my cheeks but score on supplying comic relief. "Hush, you witch!" I whispered. Her face burned pink against the boundary of her bleached blonde hair that bounced with every quiet shudder. When her snorting ensued, I knew we were in trouble.

"Bayleigh, I've gotta fevah—"

"Kins, cut your crap, and clock-in," Marcus barked, apparently not a fan of classic SNL skits. "You know I hate when you help off the clock. It's illegal. Bayleigh, get your ass up and back to work, or I'll put you on clean-up." She shot up, still super pink, fighting the giggle loop, cringing at me with bright, smiling eyes. He paused in his tracks to point a finger at both errant children before him, the band pausing like siblings to watch. At least this stole the attention from my public fail, yeah?

"Aye, aye, captain." Bayleigh's tone trembled with laughter.

"I can't hear you!" Rustin called over the mic in the stupidest signature to make the whole patronage join when Bayleigh repeated herself. Jase and I shared an incredulous smile at their blatant misbehavior, but we also knew Marcus was a sucker for anything that got the patrons going. They were now a party to our mischief. His finger pointed in our faces.

"Since I'm babysitting a bunch of children on my staff tonight, make sure you're at your best. It is obvious it's scheduled to be a big night. Big nights, bigger fish. Bigger fish, bigger tips, and bigger trouble. Should I continue, or can papa go to work?"

He didn't wait for an answer. Garrett whistled when he sauntered up to clock-in, a huge smile on his face, waiting behind another server doing the same.

She seemed less amused, and closer to Mr. Krabs. Bayleigh sneered and rolled her eyes. Oh boy, drama, drama, drama. On my way to the beer cooler, I gave her a small kick and an order to behave.

The first group of many spilled in through the front doors manned by two of our bouncers. If they were here, chaos was in the forecast, but this evening shaped up to read like a page ripped from the album of our best nights. People who hadn't trickled in since the Labor Day bash made their way over with hugs across the bar, requests for buckets of beer and shots to bump their Etch-A-Sketch buzzing. All the extra compliments on my appearance proved I'd nailed my intended mark.

Bayleigh's exuberance radiated all over her demeanor when she returned from taking orders near the stage. "We should begin our shifts with a joke every day! I'm on fire tonight, babes!" She shared a booty bump and giggle, then we hammered out the band's alcohol before five-minute call. "This crowd is great!" With that, she disappeared and reappeared before the drums with the drinks we'd made. She may have had an infectious attitude, but her flirtation wasn't enough to cancel the disappointment Jase shot my way.

Well, damn. A blush crept into my facade. *He was fine without his kiss!*

Who had time to worry about love interests when demands for booze had me scrambling in the best ways? Tuning him out was impossible when he greeted patrons. The bar went nuts with clapping, howling, whistling, and chanting. Beer bottles and mugs pounded tables in time with Mel's drumming to go with Jase's pep rally. No way he could hang onto disappointment with such motivation. Even Marcus stood against the frame of the back hallway with a huge smile on his face. Marcus's grin gleamed bright next to his dark skin, which meant I didn't need to stress over bikers and assholes. Such a relief.

"Who came out for a good time tonight?" Jase sounded over the cacophony. We bartenders cheered when he asked to see who'd brought their cash. Fists full of whatever wadded into wallets, pockets, purses and bras shot up, and Marcus put his fingers in his mouth to do the whistle that always had us covering our ears.

Jase gave his lopsided grin like a reward, turning his head to laugh away from the mic before coming back to speak. "All righty, boys and girls, I say it's time to play in the rain." The beating, chanting, hollering resumed, and the blissful sound I'd missed drained into the rush, flooding the entire bar.

Mel spun his sticks on his fingers then beat the drums. Rustin strummed his guitar. Bass chords from a guy I had yet to meet complemented the Shaun Morgan-esque crooning that signaled *Six Gun Quota* straight from Jase's sexy rasp. He was magnetic and appealing to watch as he stroked his own guitar.

"Kins, honey, I need eight margaritas! Top shelf!" one guy called, yanking me back to the here and now. "Extra salt on the side, please!"

"Babe, I need four Buds and a whiskey sour!" another yelled over the song. "God bless runners! Your legs look great tonight!"

"Thank you, sir!" I shouted into the wonderful insanity, watching Garrett twirl bottles over his wrist before running them along shot glasses like a gunslinger. He'd pocket that bottle the way a cowboy holsters a six-shooter, then he'd pull another in a blur. I made drinks beside him, and in his spare moments he'd pass them over heads I couldn't reach. When I thanked him as well, he said, "No problem, T-Rex!" and grinned back, eyes lined, top hat and suspenders in place. *What? No monocle?* Garrett had been the one to shop for my costume that fateful day when I'd met that asshole pirate. Steampunk was a way of life for him. I loved Florida freaks.

"You know, between you and Bayleigh, I should have no selfesteem left!" I teased.

"You have so much to be insecure about," he said. Two large tipsters extended money and compliments with an order to keep 'em coming. Garrett pointed at them in playful warning to keep me clean. That only led to comments about getting me dirty. Anyone could see they were playing, out for an enjoyable time that had nothing to do with having their asses beaten for sexual harassment, no harm, no foul.

Bayleigh rushed behind the bar in a fluster of wispy hair and flushed cheeks.

"Hey! Trade places with her, will ya?" Garrett called over to her, tossing her a water with an order to drink.

She nodded and recapped the bottle after she chugged.

"Garrett! They're teasing," I argued.

"Who said it was for you? I need a break from passing out your orders, and you could use time doing it yourself without trying to reach too high."

"Ass."

"Closed for business." He snickered, ordering me and a full tray out to the floor while Bayleigh called out the table numbers. I liked that he kept me from going stir-crazy behind the bar, but sometimes Garrett was protective like Jase, though flirtation came with the territory. My point was, there was no point.

Along the way, agility was my weapon against the animated talkers who flailed their drinks around with their hands, couples dancing near tables, and passersby looking for the line to the restroom to break those seals. Music vibrated the wooden planks beneath my feet while friends and familiar faces greeted in passing. A couple of vulgar comments about my buns or breasts normally came in the concoction consumed during rotations to and from the bar. Full tray, empty tray, back and forth like a worker ant. The queen was the coveted table at the front nearest to the stage, not reserved unless you had an in with the band. Since they must've been Jase's buddies, I went the extra mile.

Didn't hurt that Jase had a full view of my hustle, and I of his. When I was able to blend in, I watched as he hugged the mic with his lips and played his guitar beside Rustin, who'd join in on background lyrics. His talent was obvious. Rustin caught my eye with a smile that I returned.

Time breezed by with each song they performed, each tip to my pocket, each drink I made and served, the obstacles I avoided, and best of all, no residual pain in my ankle to haunt any of the tight-rope walking to keep from tipping trays. *What a damn good night!*

Between songs, Jase drained a mug of water, replaced the empty, and cleared his throat. He wanted his refill, and his hydration had better come from me this time. He then spoke over his loyal subjects:

"This next one is a cover from a band who knows how it goes when you're sent overseas. Though I'd have to kill all of you if I admitted the things I've done." He paused with a flirtatious grin aimed at the ladies in front of the stage. "I promise, I'd make it slow and sweet for you, girls." The men went nuts, egging on the dog. He laughed away from the mic while Bayleigh rolled her eyes. She loaded another round onto my tray while I re-hydrated.

"What gives, Bay?" She didn't give a damn about him.

"The way he watches you, then he does that, and it's like he can't pull his head from his ass long enough to go for what he wants. Why else would a headliner perform in the same place twice a week, Kins? Think of all the places downtown he could sing at during the offseason, not to mention the bank roll during the rest of the year."

"Seriously, though." Jase's voice stole any response I may have given. "Cheers to the heroes who came home under the stars and stripes. To all you who have worn and still wear the flag on your shoulders. To those who pledge allegiance to it, hang it high in your yard or at your business. And to those who stay here awaiting your soldier's return and everything that comes with the mission."

The pounding, whistling and chanting was deafening. Military of all branches stood at his urging. Marcus nodded in our direction to say shots were to go out. He hid a cringe for the moment, but his smile would split for the result.

That small hit would turn into thrice the gain.

Damn!

When I heard the opening chords to Five Finger Death

Punch's rendition of *Bad Company*, I turned and exhaled. Jase had such a smooth edge to his voice and persona when he performed this one. He'd flip that into tough and badass on the chorus like he wanted every chick to know that he could be whatever guy you wanted.

As the band got into their music, I trucked along and swatted away naughty hands that tried to steal extra shots.

Once the shots were complete, I had a lot of orders to refill and catch up on. Jase's could wait a tad longer. I stacked a tray for another table near the stage. To venture close was comparable to braving the current of the ocean on a red flag day. My knuckles turned white as I fought to keep from spilling anything as I navigated the throng. The music was so loud, I had to shout to make confirmations. That's when a guy tipped me with a twenty.

"I can't accept this!"

He nodded with a smile, even as I shook my head. "Come on, Kinsley. I insist. It's not for anyone but you!" he yelled.

"Huh?"

He flipped the bill to reveal writing on the back, then grasped my hand to wrap the money inside, curling my fingers over the top. "Call me! I'd love to pick your brain sometime." *What the hell did that mean?*

Tucking the tray with a ballerina spin in the opposite direction, I saw Jase smile down on an 8-chord break to destroy my uncertainty about letting other men down. *How did anyone have the nuts to flirt with me at all?* He was here. Watching. In ass-kicking military mode. Creeps beware.

When they finished that song, I stood holding all things that needed replenishing, and passed ice water up. He handed the drained glass back, then beer was next as Rustin, Mel and the bass player transitioned to another song. Jase extended the empty bottle just in time to grasp the mic and sing with a scratchier timbre. His eyes closed, and I became a captivated fangirl. The 'V' of sweat across his chest narrowed near his navel, soaking through his shirt like a brand of superhero waiting to reveal the true valor beneath. *Hot!* So was the temp under these stage lights. Whew. I fanned myself.

A chick beside me placed empty glasses on my tray with a request for two more Cosmopolitans. Back to business. Hustle the drinks, fight the flow, rock out with the men behaving as little boys on stage. Repeat every hour as they flew by.

An edge filtered into the air as the evening progressed, putting the staff on watch for thieves, public fornication, penis-measuring contests that risked breaking out into brawling.

"Anyone down for grown-up babysitting?" another server muttered as she passed by to clock-in. She eyed a group of men sitting at the bar. I stayed behind while Bayleigh traded with me. "Who wants to buy me a drink to help me endure my shift?" the rude bartender asked. Somehow, guys loved her mistreatment. Emasculation wasn't my thing, but whatever. She snatched money for two shots with little thanks, and not one had a problem with her attitude. Marcus never had an issue with us drinking on the job if we didn't get tanked, easier to accept a patron's generosity than to turn them down. Drunk pride being dangerous to wound and all.

She took up a tray I prepared, and once she had the table numbers, the guys' eyes followed her as she left.

Another group of masochists bites the dust.

When the band announced a break, we were so slammed I couldn't get away long enough to bring them drinks. Minutes later, an order for two shots and two beers rang out as this bartender extraordinaire manned the liquor in ways that made Garrett proud.

"WHAT KIND?" I yelled without turning.

"VODKA, PLEASE, ABSOLUT!" the customer strained over the crowd.

"BEER?" I shouted, then twirled to face him. Jase leaned over the bar with patrons buzzing around him like a hive of stirred up bees. I smiled as I grabbed the beer he drank and held the bottle on display.

"YOUR HEADLINER WOULD LIKE A DRINK! WHERE IS TONIGHT'S LUCKY BUYER?"

The lively group competed for the chance to help a brother out. I took money from a handful of random women at the end of the bar and glanced from the register to Marcus's hallway post, knowing he'd love me charging for the band's drinks rather than giving them out for free.

My smile vanished.

Intense familiarity slammed through my adrenal glands!

In the flesh, mere feet away, Complicated Moonlight stood in his signature cap with his arms crossed, leaning against the wall. He scanned the crowd like a stand-in bouncer, his lips drawn into a tight line. The light dim, the bill of his hat cast shadows that concealed the sharp details of his face, but this one wasn't happy.

When he looked over like he felt me staring, our eyes locked, and he caught me.

CHAPTER 20
KLIVE

Here a conflict, there a conflict, *everywhere* a bloody conflict if Kinsley Hayes was near. *How was she all over everything, yet unaware?*

Meanwhile, Jase Taylor pandered to the clientele packed inside the bar like cigarettes he lit up and consumed. They were his nicotine, their gleeful sounds inhaled through every breath he sucked between lyrics, and the fiery embers of his voice ate away their stressors. He was a gifted performer, but my attention waned away from him while that hot little woman delivered the strongest buzz in town. When she tended bar, alcohol wasn't necessary. Sobriety was safer.

This place wasn't my typical realm, more a dive bar at risk of going out of business years back—a lucky find shortly after I'd moved to Florida. Nightshade drank here back then, and once revamped to entice a friendlier (and cash affluent) crowd, they still hung out with a less caustic facade. Jase Taylor was old news to them, but he'd be an absolute source of power and jealousy in no time.

Three Nightshade members, my most important, wormed their ways into the crowds, blending like everyone else.

Joey wasn't Nightshade, but he was also here if I needed an extra hand with the two Inferno bikers dressed as civilians rather than donning their signature vests. They behaved, but the way the one watched Kinsley screamed ulterior motives. He communicated with his friend, whose silent vibes confirmed my suspicion.

When she breezed around the bar, her warm high met with my cold front and stirred a tempest of conflicting emotions whirling like a fearsome twister. Macabre fascination had me on edge like a storm chaser attempting to understand the thing that could kill him. Every bit as futile.

"A picture lasts longer, and it's said one's worth a thousand words. Judging by your expression, I'd bet they're all dirty." Marcus handed me a stack of paperwork. He looked over and chuckled. "You approve the uniform choice, Boss?"

"I do."

"She's cute, huh? Little Red?"

Ha! She was nothing shy of vodka-down-the-wrong-tube-sexy at work. When she ran at the beach, she wore no makeup and her hair tied up and messy. Tonight, red waves cascaded down her back, and her carnivorous eyes were sorely feline, gnawing and gnashing on the desires of men I had no right to guard against, yet here I was.

"Cute? Sure, Marcus, she's a regular kitten. Adorable, sweet, claws at the ready." She'd been vicious in the lift the first round, and last week when I'd confronted her about reporting the creep from the beach, her eyes ignited like green flames even as she played polite. I wanted to dangle toys all around to make her bat at each one with no luck, to piss her off again. She was fun to provoke. "So far, based on what I've seen, the servers are doing a great job. Place is running well, aside from these few hiccups with Mrs. Sara Scott. Honest opinion—is she prepared to quit, or does she need firing for the safety of others?"

Marcus rolled a toothpick between his lips, his good mood dimmed. "She's not coming back unless, by some miracle her issues resolve themselves." When he shot me silent askance, I shrugged.

"If it's about their marriage, I'm not risking relations between Inferno and Nightshade over personal matters. Too dangerous."

"Oh? And when these two stalking Kinsley act on their plans to deliver a threat to Sara, will you react then? When it's too late?"

"What makes you think I even care? Fire Miss Hayes for her own safety, too."

He scoffed in offense. "Klive King, do you know how valuable Kins is to your establishment? How much *Nightshade* values her service? You let it leak she might be in danger, one of them may start a war you don't want on your hands, anyway."

I turned in surprise, and he gestured out to the crowd. My first lieutenant, Eric, scoped Kinsley with a protective eye, clearly itching to haul these two snooping men out back.

"She's a figure-head around here," he said. "Taylor's in love with her, but your guys, they're loyal to the staff. Why couldn't you join that?"

Thank you, Marcus! What an interesting new twist on a pivotal part of my escape plan. Divine providence?

"How about this? I will act on her behalf under one of two conditions."

"Sara trained her. You have four-in-one with Kinsley because you had four-in-one with Sara. If we solve the problem, she can continue here—"

"What are you on about? If Sara has negative affiliations, I don't want her on the staff. Do you want to hear my conditions or not?" He waited in pointed silence. We paused as Jase pumped the Veterans. Marcus grumbled when I ordered a round of shots on the house for the servicemen and women. Why not? Jase Taylor was my candidate for replacement, so I needed to honor the things that mattered to him, this was part of that. So was Kinsley.

"See how happy your kitten is?" I grinned while he stewed.

"*My* kitten? You're not fooling anyone, King. Have fun with that since you're eyeing Taylor. How in the hell does flirting with one man's treasure make him more willing to like you? Anyway, get on with these conditions," he told me.

"If she's a weakness, I want to know. I don't need a lovesick puppy. I need a bloody hell hound. Kinsley Hayes is an excellent catalyst for feeling him out. My conditions are: if one of these Inferno pricks is planning on waiting until she's leaving to make a move, I will let Taylor act and see how evil he may be. If one leaves before, I'll go hunting."

"What's the other condition? That sounded like two, but it was one condition with two variables."

I tugged my brim lower when Kinsley headed this way. She wrapped behind the bar, this time to stay, taking wads of cash, calling charges to another server as she and Garrett made drinks as if they had a running race.

The band opted to take a break, and Jase stopped to shake hands, take pictures, listen to praise. But when the man who had taken Kinsley's hand earlier offered his up, Taylor created a space between them. *For the stalker's safety, or his own?* Marcus noticed, too.

"Looks like Taylor's trying to decide if he wants to spend his break trying to go see her or whipping this guy's ass."

I nodded. "The other condition I'd become involved is if Kinsley flat out admitted she was afraid. I'd do it for her. There. Balls out."

"So, she has a first name that he knows." He looked at me with impressed surprise. "King, I knew you had a heart in there somewhere," he teased.

"Oh, but there's a catch."

"What's that?" he shouted when the bar area grew too loud. Taylor cut a way through patrons and snagged a sacrificed space right behind where Kinsley poured rows of shots. Marcus smiled when she auctioned Taylor's drinks. Jase didn't care about the beer as much as trying to get her to notice his existence.

"For her to make a request of me, she has to know she's in danger!" I told Marcus over the volume.

When I looked up, Kinsley stared right at me. She didn't look away or blush. She had a request, all right, but the only danger on her mind was whether I'd unveil myself after our games.

Here kitty, kitty, kitty …

CHAPTER 21
KINSLEY

"Hey, Garrett, get over here and let her take a break, please?" Jase yelled. "Also, a shot of rum—she deserves it!"

Both men ignored my protest. Garrett placed a shot glass in my fingers and warned of no chasers to follow. In other words, no spitting the liquor inside a bottle. I downed the rum, then Garrett handed me a cocktail napkin to wipe the dribble.

"I didn't spill," I said. Garrett peered around my back, then scoffed. "What?"

"It wasn't for the rum. It was for the drool over the guy you're scoping as Romeo busted his ass to make it over here to spend his break with you. Loyalty, Kins."

He earned a slap to his bicep, and I avoided looking at the cloak-and-dagger gentleman. "We aren't together, you brat, so I am free to scope whomever I want."

"Touché, grasshopper. I forgive you, but one at a time." At least he grinned, then ordered that I take fifteen and stay close to Jase. "No questions, just frigging go. I've got work to do."

"Okay, jeez." I turned to Jase once more. *I will not scope the guy in the cap!* "Hold on, and I'll come around, okay?" Jase shook his head no, stood to his full height, and hoisted me over the bar as I giggled in shock. The drunken entourage surrounding us erupted in dirty catcalls. *Yikes.*

"Baby, they are harmless. You're safe. Now, turn around and put your feet on top of mine the way you had to do with that two-step," he said at my ear. I cupped a laugh. His arm was strong at my waist, the other came out to shove naughty hands while we duck-walked toward the stage through the rowdy mass. He didn't give them a tough time since he claimed responsibility for their...*enthusiasm.* Is this what busy nights were always like for him? Who cared? All I sensed was the heat where our bodies connected! The spiritual warnings were barely audible in the buzz of electrical charge.

When we got to the stage, I mingled with the band. The new bass player, Dan, though shy, introduced himself to me and the three women who'd glued themselves to Mel. After shaking a few hands, they resumed. Rustin had his arm around a pretty waist as he drank a beer on the steps and added to their conversation, careful not to leave her out. Mr. Taylor, however, situated himself apart.

"Hey you!" I raised my voice and faced him with an elbow digging at his ribs. "Should I go back to work and let you partake? You're so quiet!" He grinned down in answer, shaking his head, his brown hair dark and wet near his scalp. The rest of his tresses tangled with his eyelashes so that he tossed them like an afterthought.

"Kins, I swear, one day we will drill it into your head you're my favorite girl!" he yelled. "If I can spend my break with you, why waste it on anyone else?" There was such a legit notion in his face, I had to glance away. His turn to elbow my ribs. He smiled like he didn't need sunglasses to shield his eyes from the blinding inferno erupting in my cheeks. "Do you want to go back to work? I mean, if this makes you uncomfortable...?"

Gotta appreciate a man who allows a tinge of his vulnerability to mix with yours. His relieved laugh at my emphatic head shake added a tingle to my palms as they wrapped around the edge of the stage while I hoisted myself to sit upon the wood surface.

"Excuse me." He leaned over—*against* me—to reach his beer.

The insane intimacy was in that my thighs were apart, him standing between them, and when he lifted back up, he didn't move his hips away. Just dipped the bottle to his lips then placed the sweating Bud near my right hip, his other hand rested beside the left. Inner conflict raged with the inappropriate desires that sparked to life. Pretending I was unaffected and focused on the stories he told of various other gigs, was futile until the others joined. About ten minutes in, cackling at their tales came as easy as the desire to let down my defenses.

"Gosh, I pray I'm never in one of these!" I teased and smacked Rustin in the stomach for what he'd added about some chick. He gave me a line of flattering bull, stole my hand without letting me pull my fingers away, and asked about the small calluses to distract me. As he resumed talking, his fingertips played over them. Jase had no issue, so I resigned to allow Rustin's flirtation.

The crowd's impatience grew too obvious to ignore, so before leaving them, I produced the Valentine card that had been on the calla lilies. "Will you read this and tell me if you recognize it as a song?" Rustin snapped the cardstock from my grasp first, but Jase swiped the poem, his eyes narrowed. When he looked back up, his right eyebrow rose.

"Kins, this looks like it came from a floral shop. Someone send you flowers, baby?"

I chewed my cheek as if I didn't know he was the guilty

party (thank you, Michael Taylor). "Well, these calla lilies came in a mix of a ton of other stuff...." I grinned like an excited idiot thrilled to get something.

"A ton of other stuff, eh?" Jase pointed the card at me with his big brother authority. Great. "I'm gonna investigate this since it seems familiar, but you need to watch the ones that don't leave information. Never know who's watching you, okay?" *Um, a dig at my cloaked secret admirer asshole pirate, perhaps?* "Mm-kay, creepy. Thanks, daddy." There was a reflective smart-ass in his grin. He licked his lips.

"Daddy isn't my style, baby, but we can see how things pan out when the moment presents itself. For you, sweet Kins, I'll keep an open mind." With a salacious gasp, I slapped his arm that rose to high-five Rustin.

"You, sir, are far too presumptuous. Time for you to go back on, and for me to mix drinks."

"Uh, uh, uh...not so fast, woman. Your first order of duty is to accommodate these poor patrons who've had to endure my off-key songs because *you* never kissed me." Jase gave a mournful look at the antsy crowd and placed a bereft fist over his lips at the travesty. I cackled once more and reached out to pull his hand away from his mouth.

"*I* didn't kiss *you*, huh? So now we've switched?"

"Well, you kissed me that other time, so I figured you'd want to again." He shut up when I grabbed both of his cheeks. His expression transitioned to a kaleidoscope of hope, surprise, victory, all manner of uncertainty, but he leaned in without hesitation. He expected my lips on his and groaned when they planted instead on his cheek. His chest expanded as my kiss lingered. I felt his lungs deflate when I disconnected. The desire to try for more showed in how he licked his lips and looked at mine. Gosh, I wanted him to, but he restrained his temptation.

I vaulted off the stage. He grabbed my hand and tugged me back with an urgency in his expression.

"Kins, any requests?"

We held eye-contact for a beat. "Surprise me," I challenged and walked away before he responded. *How deep would the shallow Jase Taylor push himself when he wanted something?* A Navy SEAL had more willpower than I'd seen of him with women.

The pirate was right. I was tired of boys and empty flirtation and watching my best friend's brother stay the epitome of such when there was more. Why not discover whether he could put his money where his mouth was? The worst that would happen was I'd end up thinking of him as shallow as I did now.

By the time I went back behind the bar to resume my shift, I noticed the ball cap guy disappeared. Jase downed a bottle of water while the band resumed their places on stage. Recapping the empty, Jase took to the mic. "All right, all right! Sorry, I broke longer than usual, but have you guys *seen* that cute bartender?"

I slapped hands over my face. *He didn't just do that!* Bayleigh knocked my fingers away and forced me to endure the roar in agreement.

"So then, you forgive me?" he asked them, yeah, they forgave him.

"For those of you who may not realize, I *love* surprising people."

Oh, no! No, no, no, no, NO!

"I consider myself a humble man." He couldn't keep a straight face in the ensuing crap-calling. His guitar strap lifted over his head. The instrument rested against his hip, and his left-hand pat his chest in faux sincerity. "When I get a request from a beautiful woman, my humility takes the back seat to please the requestor, especially when she wants a surprise. I need audience participation for this song. Anyone ever work a tambourine?"

Good grief—about every female in this place.

This man! Careful what you wish for.

He pointed, and three clamoring chicks tripped over each other in a tizzy before the victor trotted on stage in heels too high for her to pull off a seamless strut. Okay, she was amusing and impossible to hate for trying to look cute, but after that cat spat, she was a hot mess. She straightened her dress and smoothed her hair as he held the tambourine out to her with the same humor on his face. "Congratulations! You're tonight's lucky contestant," he teased. She leaned his way to take the instrument, eyes all a bat, breasts and booty bubbled.

Jase played indifferent even as he moved close to ask her a question. *Hey, baby, how'd you like to shake this for me later?* One could pray my imagination scripted worse than reality. Whatever he asked, she nodded with a huge grin.

He turned to the rest of the group, and said something inaudible, pulled the mic up to his mouth, and his free hand pointed at me. *Dafuq!*

"Kinsley, baby, this one is for you!" The crowd cheered as the tambourine shook. Dan strummed the familiar bass chords to Jet's *Are You Gonna Be My Girl*. Mel joined in on the drums, Rustin shared a fist bump and a huge smile with Jase, then came in right on time while Jase *screamed* into the mic!

"You're kidding me!" I cheesed at Bayleigh.

She set about dancing as she served drinks behind the bar. "Who'd have ever pegged *him* for a British Invasion, yeah? Think it's a passive jab to the beautiful British Moonlight?"

"Bayleigh, Jet is Aussie," I said with an eye roll.

"Hey, I'm talking style and I have a point."

"It's an impressive performance, but I don't think it has anything to do the the Brit."

"I'll agree that I could be reaching, but I don't think he's joking with the lyrics!" she shouted to be heard over Jase's fanfare.

Jase winked at me, producing a fit of giggles. Bayleigh giggled along, because he was such an animated fool all the while—changing the lyrics to 'cute black shoes' and the color of hair to red, counting off the numbers with his fingers, and a *'but you won't date a single man, yeah!'* to replace the debacle in the radio version. Bayleigh was so right, and this naughty headliner made no mysteries as he grabbed his heart because I kept shooting him down.

She rubbed her throat in empathy. "He's gonna need more water after this!"

"For sure!" I grinned and tried to focus on serving.

The whole band rocked the stage like this venue was much larger and their names glowed in flashing lights. We're talking dancing with the mic stand idiocy! The level of passion and fun they threw into their performance was contagious, so there was no choice but to rock out with Bayleigh and confirm myself as the one he was singing to when Captain Obvious left the building the more alcohol these patrons consumed.

The relationship questions were awkward. What should I say? We were not together, but was that my fault or Jase's? What would happen if—*nope*—the brakes slammed hard on those thoughts.

The most rational option was to enjoy the moment. The adoration from smiling too much gave me away. Jase was so silly, confident, sexy, talented, take your pick! After that screaming, his voice would be the raspy I loved.

When he went to his knees, flipping the damp hair from his eyes, the last lyrics of the song screeched across the speakers and his finger rested in my direction. Pregnant silence ensued where the normal applause would have erupted, and my throat seized in a panic! *Holy hell, did they expect me to answer that question? Now?!* Instead, I settled for whistling between two of my fingers and cheering as that 'woo!' girl. The bar followed while Jase picked himself up off the stage with a knowing corner of his mouth smiling at me like he'd accepted a challenge—he *wasn't* backing down.

CHAPTER 22
KINSLEY

Bayleigh leaped to my side to fill a mug with foamy brew. "You can't avoid him forever. He asked you out." She was right, but I stalled.

"Bayleigh, he sang a song. What he's paid to do. It's common knowledge he is a chronic flirt. This buys them more tips." Glancing at the stage, Jase studied me while downing another bottled water, then took a swig of beer. He turned to talk to the band.

"Oh, yeah. You're the flavor of the evening," Garrett added. He dipped between us for some cherries, my attention back on making cocktails. "And Bayleigh isn't into that tatted punk on the drums, either." She and Mel had been, er...eye-*loving*...each other for most of the night. Garrett took an extra cherry to toss and catch with his mouth for the ladies he wooed, then another, and they all oohed and awed when he produced both stems tied together.

"Show off," we grumbled.

"Say what you want, see what you will," Garrett called as Jase spoke to the chick onstage with the tambourine again.

"Women are too hard or dense. What the hell does a guy gotta do for a date?" He looked at the ladies in question.

Jase cleared his throat over the mic and curtailed the lecture Garrett prepared to give, hushing the captive audience along with him. "All right. Just so there's no confusion, that song was for Kinsley Hayes. This next one is for the redhead working behind the bar."

I gasped and looked up with slack-jaw shock as the band covered Buckcherry's *Next to You*. Jase's smirk was full of vindictive confirmation as he threw in with the rest and started singing. Well, hell! Garrett leaned in to pop off.

"Enough, mister!" I snapped in his face and commanded him to, "Shut it!" He and Bayleigh fist bumped while I rolled my eyes and hustled drinks. Marcus came to help at the liquor counter, happy and irritated all at the same time as he snatched bottles for me.

"I'll say this for you, kid. You sure can reel 'em in." I did a double take when realizing this wasn't a compliment.

"What the hell? Are you insulting Jase?"

"Garrett, call the other two bouncers to assist Gus and Jarrell with this crowd. Line's out the door, and at this rate, the damn fire marshal might walk in and close us down."

"Since when does the fire marshal care about this place?"

Marcus ignored my questions. "We've got two brawls on our hands, and one cat fight. It's a *Monday* night. Shouldn't happen until next week!"

Garrett agreed and set about following orders. Jase was making a romantic fool of himself to my right. Marcus frustrated with me on my left. Bayleigh at my back trying to keep from stepping on toes, and tipsy jokers sat in front of me. Talk about surrounded.

"Kins!" Marcus addressed me. "You know I like Taylor.

Means you're doing an excellent job, but as soon as Romeo finishes his little stunt, you are going home."

"But I—"

His hand sliced the air between us, cutting me off clean. *Did he seem too liberal with granting time off as of late?* Under normal circumstances, he was the exact opposite. *Why this recent change?*

"Kins, don't argue. I'm not mad, want to keep you safe with all the attention."

Chewing my cheek, I tried reading between the lines regarding what he *didn't* say. This was the second time he'd sent me home early in the past month.

"This about that creep from Inferno who harassed Sara? The guy who gave me crap about men on motorcycles? Is he in here tonight? Because I'm not making him a damn Rusty Nail. I'd rather hammer a rusty nail to his forehead."

Marcus chuckled. "What if he was? Does that scare you?"

"What?" He almost seemed like he was goading me for a certain response. "If he has bad intentions, yeah, I guess it does," I sputtered. "I mean, Rustin pointed out how we both have red hair, how in low light I might be mistaken—" I broke off. "Wait. Is this about Inferno, or is it that guy with the ball cap that keeps watching me? You guys were talking, maybe you warned him or something? I mean, he's never here, then suddenly he's here on the regular. Garrett claims he's come in over the years, but this is the first I'm seeing him...." My mouth ran away on tangents meant to provoke him as we shouted over one another. That guy wasn't the creep, nor did he creep me out, but damn!

A cat call shifted our attention down to the end. "Always great service, Kinsley. You know just how to light a fire, darlin'. You have my number," a dude called then disappeared out of our back entrance. Marcus growled and narrowed his eyes at me after staring him down. *Ugh! That was the last thing I needed right now!*

"The man in the hat *isn't* a danger to you. He recognized you from the paper, that's all. Happens all the time. I think it's obvious anytime you're featured we get perverts."

"So, he *is* a pervert, then?" We both knew Complicated Moonlight wasn't who I'd accused him of being, but Marcus was hiding something.

"Kinsley Hayes, I'm warning you now, if you don't stop, you'll hear a fat lady joining Taylor's singing." My lips clamped shut. Marcus had never threatened to fire me before.

"I'm going to work the floor. Bayleigh cover me?" I asked in disgruntled frustration.

"No, young lady, you're behind the bar for the duration," Marcus ordered. "It's my job to keep you safe, it's your job to make drinks. Two on the end are empty. Bayleigh, take the floor, and Kins back to work."

Jase stole away the fit I prepared to throw when he wrapped that song, and the bar came alive with rhythmic clapping and stomping while chanting for more.

"Oh, you want more? Don't we all?" Jase quirked his eyebrows at me, causing a heart rush and a little smile in the mix of my pissy. He turned and cued Rustin, who busied with changing guitars as he nodded. "Give this go-go girl a round of applause and drinks for working that tambourine!" She bowed after he kissed her cheek and sent her fluttering off stage with a delightful story and more cocktails than she could drink in one night. "This gem goes out to my sister's best friend, wherever she is."

I bit my lip through a bigger smile as I split lime wedges for martini glasses.

"Who is his sister, and is he talking 'bout this redhead on

the last song?" a white-girl-wasted drawl shouted to Marcus. "I'm so confused!"

He pinched the toothpick he chewed and arched an eyebrow at me. "No, he's talking about someone else, and he doesn't have a sister. You must've heard him wrong!" Marcus pronounced each syllable like she was hard-of-hearing. I laughed at her scrunched face, tilted head, duck lips and Marcus held his arm up so I could snuggle in for a side hug. "See," he hissed by my ear. "Crazies don't only come with male appendages."

"Point taken, boss."

There was an anticipatory lull when Rustin spoke into the mic, "I apologize for being rusty." He paused for us to laugh at his pun, then said, "Here goes nothing." All clapping for him came down with the hand he lowered inch-by-inch until their volume was nil. A cough was the only sound when Mel beat the drums on an introduction. Rustin's pick pinched between his fingers while he prayed over his instrument, willing the guitar's compliance, then the sliver of ivory metered out the iconic *Eruption* of Van Halen's, *You Really Got Me*. Both hands worked like simultaneous brushes scrolling in different directions to paint the same harmonic picture. He chopped at each note but held that guitar like a reverent man in love.

Jase gripped the mic and watched his friend instead of me until silence hung again as Rustin's final note laid over the heads watching.

Jase strummed his own guitar, and the band joined him and Rustin. The performing prankster disappeared to morph into a man on a mission. He sang these words like meaningful facts, natural, effortless, and alternated between holding the mic between both hands and going at his guitar here and there.

I assisted patrons while I watched Jase more so than the earlier two songs, but the ghost of crushes past played memories in my mind as my body went through the motions. History swirled around Tyndall's house. I tried recalling signs her brother may have shown back then. No, that was dreaming for the dorky romantic I'd been as an idiotic teen. The reality of how much I should enjoy Jase's show for *that* part of me slapped my insecurity out of the picture! *This was amazing!*

"Your boyfriend is so hot! Hope you don't mind us saying so!"

"Kinsley, you're so lucky. How long have you two been together?"

"Is this what it takes to win a date with Kinsley Hayes?"

"What about the roses I sent you?"

"Who knew Jase Taylor was so romantic!"

"Did he plan this?"

"Does he sing to you when you are alone, too?"

"If you'd worked on a karaoke night, I would have done this for you! C'mon! Just a date. Just one date!"

"No fair! You've tied each other down!"

"I thought you wanted to have coffee."

"Does this mean Jase is off the market, or can I still sleep with him?"

"Should I get my panties out of his truck, then?"

Okay, I admit, I imagined the last two questions there, but interviews I'd given to papers and podcasts for track or scholastic achievements weren't as intense. Factor in the crowd had standing-room-only with both Marcus and Garrett taking and passing drinks as fast as I could make them. Faces blurred in the lucrative mayhem, and Marcus's expression fished for gratitude about ordering me home early.

Wait—*coffee? Roses!* Record skip! *Had Moonlight come to own up?*

"Marcus, did you see the person who mentioned coffee?"

"Huh?"

Applause erupted when the song finished, and I clapped, flattered by all that was happening, but *he was here!* Oh, dammit all! What a mess this evolved into.

Jase placed his hand on Rustin's shoulder. "I can't take all the credit on that one. Please give it up for my best friend and amazing guitar player, Rustin Keane, ladies and gentlemen!" Soon Jase and Mel wouldn't be the only ones with a following here. Rustin fanned himself for more with a huge grin on his face.

"All right, enough about him. Let's return to the real star. We're slowing it down."

Even though Marcus asked me to repeat my question, my throat was too busy closing as Jase set a stool near the mic and sat down. An acoustic guitar replaced the electric he'd been playing on. Rustin placed his onto a stand and grabbed the tambourine while adjusting the other mic stands. Mel came around to sit in front of his drum kit with a little bongo between his legs. He lowered the mic until he greeted everyone and reminded the crowd that 'he was just the drummer in the background'. Dan kept his bass guitar but shared a mic with Rustin.

Hmm ....

Jase cleared his throat. "This next one goes out to the girl I had a crush on in high school."

"Nope, I'm done," I said and tossed my towel to the bar. I could handle no more. This wasn't real. This was a successful publicity stunt. "Marcus, can I go now?" I felt ready to have a panic attack. I didn't want that *Carrie* moment when I learned this was all an elaborate hoax.

"Shhh...let the man finish. If he hurts you, we'll take care of it," he teased, flexed his bicep. He spun me by my shoulders and kept his hands there like reassurance while I waited for whatever Jase would say next, whatever he would play.

"A girl who starred in my thoughts, if you know what I mean, and distracted me anytime she came around. When I listen to this song, I think of her, and when I sing along, she's who I'm singing about."

"I can't," I whispered.

"You *are*." Marcus tightened his grip like he needed to keep me from bolting.

"Ladies and gentlemen," Jase continued, "I'm sure by now you can guess who I am talking about, but this one is for the adorable redhead with the short hair, braces, the cutest blush, and the most beautiful smile all the while." His eyes held mine as he took a long drink of water. Mel counted to four for the band, then beat his wrist on the bongo. Rustin had something small in his right hand that sounded like a rain maker he began to shake while simultaneously hitting the tambourine against his knee with his left hand. Jase started strumming a song I absolutely loved.

Tears prickled, and Marcus kept me in place. This was overwhelming, and too much of a good thing almost hurt.

A rendition of Mr. Big's *To Be With You* floated through air that had grown stale with the stench of sweaty pheromones and booze. The whole band harmonized with Jase's rasp that melted into these lyrics so well, but as he pulled from his stomach to belt his vocals as they climbed in volume and passion, the voice that delivered rock and blues could steal the hearts of angels. How did mine stand a chance?

Slow-dancing couples took to the floor where lusty women had been minutes before.

Drops of perspiration rained down the sides of his stubbled cheeks, and his shirt molded to his torso. Every lash of his fingers against his guitar flexed his biceps. He was beautiful, each word that poured from his mouth drew straight from his heart like a tightened bow and shot like an arrow that pierced mine with bittersweet pain. Jase didn't sing ballads too often, so catching one was comparable to trapping a butterfly in a jar.

Did Tyndall tell her brother of my love for 80s rock and my associated weakness for bad boys being sweet?

Jase grinned and held my eyes while telling me he wanted to be with me, been waiting in line to be with me, and hoped I felt the same. Part of me knew he was taking a punch at the pain my ex-boyfriend from high school, Jack, had caused me, and I knew now while Jase sang that he'd wanted me then.

A flash of his brown irises colored in pain during what I'd thought the worst moment of my life played on a private reel with his voice as the soundtrack:

"I'm sorry, Jase. I'm so ashamed. This is nothing compared to what you have seen and gone through. Please, forgive me for my petty, childish shit."

"I appreciate that. Kinsley, it's okay to feel pain. I don't care who you are, what you've been through, we all have our scope and tolerance levels. If the shit hurts, it hurts. We can't help how we feel when it happens, right? Is there some gauge that says having your heart ripped out should be less painful than death? It's like death, right? In its own way?"

"I feel like I will die. What is left of me? Who am I? What do I have to offer? What is there to look forward to now?"

He'd rushed to capture me, and he'd carried me to safety as the brave soldier home on leave he'd been those years ago.

Real friends let you crash and kept you protected like a safety belt. They didn't take the belt off and allow you to slam through the windshield, shattering to irreparable pieces. They didn't deny that the crash was imminent. Jase had buckled me in, never feeding me BS lines to lessen the impact, but I'd always assumed he'd comforted me out of obligation to his sister. How crazy. Even reflecting on that day put a debilitating lump inside my throat.

Oh, Jase. Dammit. I swiped stupid tears from under my eyes.

Bayleigh looked at me like I was in for trouble. I widened my eyes in agreement as she handed me a tissue to sop up the mascara streams.

I bore the full weight of the reverent stillness when he finished holding the final note for an awe-striking amount of time. He sat unmoving, and the bar sat with him.

CHAPTER 23
KLIVE

The next half-hour of my life consisted of watching Jase Taylor pine in ways that showed the patronage in the bar that Kinsley Hayes was more than a one-night conquest. As a red-blooded male, seeing was believing. Landing that woman would take more than positioning himself between her thighs and her kissing his cheek.

He was a dumb-ass on that stage, I'd give him that. A clever way to win her over. Even *I* laughed a few times, so who blamed her for the gorgeous smile? Didn't keep me from wanting to knock her off her certainty about him while knocking her off her feet for my own. If he wanted her, let's see him prove the hell out of his worth.

Where his friend, Rustin Keane, fit into that mix would have to flesh itself out, but I hadn't missed their private communication during the break. Kinsley cackled the whole time, never suspecting that Deputy Keane had dropped his companion to grab her hand as a passive threat to the Inferno voyeur I edged closer to now.

Eric, Joey, and I passed one another, shifting and

communicating. Seemed Marcus's wish may come true. An Inferno biker signaled another, then Gustav flagged me. Joey walked out the door with eyes on Kinsley's vehicle in the lot. Eric followed the biker. That left me with tonight's most wanted. The remaining two Nightshade members gazed at me to ask if I needed aid. I shook my head.

Marcus eyed the guy and did his best to keep Kinsley distracted, but he was praying this stalker would give me the excuse to kill him. When the wanker leaned against the hallway in the same place Marcus and I had been standing not so long ago, possession sizzled my veins. From there, you could see behind the bar and every rise Kinsley made onto the tips of her toes, the muscles in her legs, the way her shirt rose and exposed her midriff when she reached for the glasses. He checked her out like ticking off an itemized list of things to get off on. I ticked off murder tactics.

"...as soon as Romeo finishes his little stunt, you are going home," Marcus said loud enough that the bloody stalker and I heard. I glared, but Marcus sent that scowl right back while Kinsley gave him a slurry of attitude. At least he stepped in to block the bastard's view.

"Is this about that guy who harassed Sara? Is he in here tonight?" she fired off.

The Inferno voyeur enjoyed a subtle laugh of sick victory! The prick wanted to die. My jaw clenched at the bullshit stunt Marcus had pulled, but he kept going.

"Why, does that scare you?" he asked. Fabulous. Her expression softened, and her eyes grew to that same plea that made me go after her when she'd fled into the stairwell. When I shouldn't have, yet here I was—again—chasing shit that upset her!

"If he has bad intentions, yeah, I guess it does. I mean, Rustin pointed out how we both have red hair, how in low light I might be mistaken—" she broke off. "Wait. Is this about Inferno, or is it that guy with the ball cap that keeps watching me? You guys were talking, maybe you warned him or something?" Off she went on an insulting tirade.

A whistle wrenched my attention off her to narrow on the asshole. "Always great service, Kinsley. You know just how to light a fire," the stalking asshole hollered. "You have my number."

Marcus glared at him, then me before settling on 'Little Red' like the whole incident had been her fault.

As I watched the prick stalk down the employee hallway, Kinsley prattled off, changing tones and attitudes and opinions faster than the wind shifts. She knew better. If she was spooling up, she feared something, and was likely taking aim at me for what that creep had just done.

I texted Joey.

What's your 20?

Outside smoking

*vaping

Eyes on Inferno?

One's watching her car. He's hostile 💀

Let's deploy 👀

Even if Taylor stopped performing right this instant, he'd still not arrive at her place in time to stop the stalker. I shot Marcus a confirming look and listened to him argue with this little woman, back to a bratty girl.

Perhaps my anger surged too strong, or was the idea of those fingerless-gloved hands on my girl just too damn much? If I rushed after him, I'd make a mistake in this mental fog.

Another song *should* have made me jealous but didn't. Jase's stunt gave me a chance to think, to calm, to plan before I allowed emotion to lead my better judgment.

When the patrons at the bar fired questions at Kinsley, I threw some of mine in there to torment her the way she tormented me. "What about the roses I sent you? I thought you wanted to have coffee."

She turned to Marcus with genuine panic and disappointment written all over her face to ask if he'd seen me. Good. She deserved the torment. Taylor may have been gunning for her heart, but *I* was about to *pull my gun* in her honor. Let's see Jase do that. Then I'd consider whether he loved her. Until then, time for the gloves to come off.

Marcus looked my way. I tipped my hat and stormed out the back door.

KINSLEY'S NEIGHBORHOOD epitomized the American Dream, well-to-do houses, manicured yards, basketball goals in driveways, flowerbeds that won best yard of the month awards, jogging paths. Her family's Craftsman style home, with the cliché white picket fence and porch swing, slept at the top of a curving incline with a panoramic view of the park. Large oaks draped in moss flanked either side of the residence and dotted the playground in front.

I parked on the other side of the playground and inspected the sets of French doors lined by Juliet balconies through my night vision scope. So far, no signs of life. Neither the three balconies in the main house nor the two at the front of the garage apartment showed a single shift in the darkness or the flicker of a light beyond their sheer curtains. No cars in their circle drive. No movement for the past ten minutes except for a randy couple kissing at the top of the playground slide.

A large branch hung close to the garage apartment Kinsley took residence in. The good and bad thing about hundred-year-old oaks, they withstood weight; a man's weight was nothing. A randy boyfriend would scale that tree like a cat, so an Inferno firefighter could nail that entry point in seconds. I would not do the same. Too predictable.

I reached into my back seat and shrugged into a college Letterman jacket sporting the surname of a frat jerk that owed Nightshade money. Next, I pocketed my Sig and its silencer, snapped on black nitrile gloves, and tucked a garrote away, just in case.

Time to go to work, and fast. Kinsley's stalker may not have been foolish enough to try anything tonight, but as I made my way past the couple with nothing more than a 'sup man,' I felt that intuitive tingle.

My eyes narrowed at the edge of the road, looking up to the window roughly two feet away from the thick branch beside the garage. The sill appeared open at the bottom. Curtains inside billowed with the breeze every so often. Confirmation that Kinsley Hayes needed a hard lesson in protecting herself.

I made a sharp right at the pavement until the park was no longer visible. One advantage of their lot being over-sized, on a curve, the next-door neighbors' homes faced away from the property on both sides. When I saw no traffic on the street or camera systems on the neighbor's house, I circled back and traversed the outdoor staircase leading to her front door. A knowing sensation lifted the hairs on my arms, the back of my neck, prickling my scalp. I wasn't alone. I practically smelled the unmistakable stench of nervousness culling from inside.

Kinsley's shift didn't end for another forty-five minutes. More than enough time to pistol-whip and haul the prowler to the Rover under the guise of a drunkard needing a ride in case a neighbor noticed. The dirty work would continue elsewhere.

Reaching for my kit, the thought dawned that I may not even need to pick the lock. *Please let me be wrong!*

The cool metal doorknob revolved beneath my glove, confirming my worst fears for Kinsley.

Every murderous instinct I'd restrained for the last two weeks came undone.

CHAPTER 24
KINSLEY

Marcus grabbed my attention.

"Kins, you can stay. I'm sorry I took my stress out on you." My manager looked down at me while I wondered what the hell had changed his mind. Bayleigh's hand gave another supportive squeeze before she mixed a gin and tonic. Marcus lifted his finger to signal Jase this had better be the final song of this stunt before he got back to his normal performance sets.

"You want one more?" Jase asked the intoxicated assembly, understanding. They cheered in answer to Jase's broken silence. Deep emotion still swam in his eyes, but they lit with enthusiasm. "This last song is from a band I cover often called Seether. This goes out to the only woman who holds my attention whenever I'm here, whether or not I am working," he said. He gazed at spots nowhere near me that had me searching in curiosity. "A woman I hope will at least give me a date after tonight. Perhaps even one day her heart." He stared at me that time. The resounding, "aww!!!" from every female in the bar, including Bayleigh, made me smile. Made me nerve-eating nauseous, too.

"Bayleigh Blue! What has gotten into you?" I turned away from Jase to pin her traitorous googly eyes.

"What? I'm still a woman, aren't I? If you don't give him a date, you will come off like a total bitch!" She pointed at him while her hands crossed over her chest. "Never thought I'd say this about that man, but he's *smart.*"

She was right. I'd look awful if I turned him down. When I spun to face him once more, he gave that lopsided grin, melting the trouble he caused down the drain. I loved when Jase performed anything by Seether, but what song could such a hardcore band have in their albums to convey anything sweet enough to dedicate? Was I about to be offended?

"Song's called *Never Leave.*" Jase said. The electric guitar was back to replace the acoustic, pedal near Jase's perched feet. Mel took his regular spot at the drum kit. Rustin tapped his toes to the counts his bestie measured with each note he strummed to life, then he joined in as Jase took to the mic in his sexy rasp. This one didn't have the same sweetness. More a rough vulnerability and angst. Interesting shift. He scratched along in his sultry signature about being nervous, showing excitement and wanting more, like the Valentine. *Oh! Like the Valentine! The poem! Loud and clear. Never Leave. Aw!*

"And...*there's* his permission to pass Go and collect." Bayleigh elbowed me on her way past as she worked the bar. I shook my head and stood rooted while Jase sent a knowing smile and owned up to sending *that* bouquet. His plea was a powerful appeal to never leave his company, that I'm the one who keeps him excited and begging for more, but always at bay, that he would keep trying for me. He feared putting his heart on the line.

Risk was worth the reward.

Well, I was out of excuses. All those miserable shifts of Jase Taylor treating me like his little sister had been to push me to a safe distance. How had this fine specimen had a crush on the bad haircut, brace-face Kinsley Hayes in this alternate universe I'd stumbled into?

The song grew as heavy as my reality. *What if this didn't work out?* Tyndall had acted so cavalier, but say I wrecked Jase's heart, or, more probable, he shattered mine? Where would that put her? Or this friendship I'd always counted on with Jase?

The song ended with a single note wafting through the air, and once more, silly Jase had left in favor of the contemplative deep thinker.

He studied me, helpless to have to go into requests for his next set without seeking me out. Part of me wanted to run through the crowd like the end of a corny chick flick and tackle him with a million yeses. But did I only want him because he was a teenaged crush Freshman year? Because he was gorgeous and sexy and everything wrong? Because my father seemed okay with the idea?

There was much to consider.

I untied my apron, counted my till and tips, divvied them up to share with the bar-backs and dish washers in the kitchen. Marcus walked up as I grabbed my bag from the locker area.

"What are you doing, Kins? You can stay. You should."

"I'm leaving, Marcus. I don't want to give him an answer because everyone expects me to. He deserves better than that. When I respond, he'll know it's real and not for show."

"I can respect that, Little Red. Pray about it, or whatever you do," he told me in awkwardness, but I loved his thought.

When I opened the back door, he followed me while insisting I could stay, even as a patron, adding that I should face my fears. *Did he want me to give Jase a chance? What happened to that junk about making Taylor work his butt off?*

"No, Marcus. That crowd is crazy. Besides, with the

Inferno stuff going on with Sara, it's best I leave while the bar is full. You were right earlier, and I'm sorry I gave you crap."

He sighed and ran a palm over his forehead, then jogged ahead of me. Jarrell paused his bouncer duties at the door to join us. His hand touched the small of my spine while he paid strict attention to everything.

"You guys okay?" They walked me the entire way to my car, making me paranoid.

"Kins, I don't want you scared. I promise we'll talk, but not yet. I'm still working some things out," Marcus assured me like a father pushing away questions from a five-year-old. "For now, save your energy so you can keep running from Taylor's hot pursuit." *There he is ladies and gents! What the heck?*

"I'm not running! I'm thinking. There's a difference."

Jarrell's laugh echoed over the empty vehicles. I almost demanded an explanation, but my mind was so heavy, I conceded. Marcus's laughter joined. "Right, when you earn *that* metal, you show it so I can slap him upside the head if the rock is too small."

"Back and forth. Honestly, you guys need to make up your minds. Nice pun on the medal, by the way."

Marcus asked me to stay once more, but I shut the door on further arguments and watched him in the rearview until the bar faded.

CHAPTER 25
KLIVE

The air inside the small apartment should have hollowed with dead silence, but the quiet filled my ears like cotton. I sensed an invisible presence occupying space, shifting and blocking the ticking of a bedroom clock and the conditioned air heaving through a vent.

The front door pressed closed at my back. I released the knob with the same calculated millimeters that I had used to open the portal, assessing obstacles while my eyes adjusted to the darkness. In the living area, golden light from a neighboring streetlamp spilled through sheer curtains over the two sets of French doors. Two couches covered in pillows and throw blankets faced each other, and a vase with dead flowers adorned the coffee table between them.

To the left, blue digits on the microwave displayed the wrong time. A curtain was drawn over the window above the sink. Dirty dishes lined the length of the counter. The kitchen island filled with mail and papers, a laptop, candles, and the crystal vase from the roses I'd gifted her for Valentine's Day.

The interior door beside the refrigerator leading to the

garage below locked tight at both intervals. *Sure, love, secure the entry that doesn't matter....*

I joined the pistol with the silencer and crept toward the shallow hallway. Movement! I jolted into a bathroom, nearly tripping as I wrapped my foot in a pair of panties!

Me. That was *my* own bloody reflection in a full-length mirror at the end of the hall. *Tosser!*

At least the shower curtain wasn't drawn. No one hiding there.

The washer and dryer across the hall sat between open accordion doors. Kinsley's laundry flooded the floor. I bent and yanked the knickers from my ankle and tossed them back into the mess.

This meant the wanker lurked behind one of two cracked bedroom doors. Each flanked my reflected image. Carpet absorbed a repeated struggle with another pair of Kinsley's obstinate undergarments! *This bloody woman and her laziness!*

Rather than tossing the booby-trap, I hung onto the bra. My patience expired! Instead of kicking in doors, I strode to her front entry and ripped the door open with a resounding slam shut a second later. "Kinsley, baby!" I called with no accent, mimicking Taylor. "Did I beat you here? You left your door unlocked." Unwilling to dance in the dark, I flipped the light switch that supplied enough glow to illuminate the living, kitchen, and hallway.

With the gun behind my leg, I marched straight to both doors and kicked the right open. Her study rested empty except for a corner desk and the normal at-home office supplies, sleeping desktop computer. The curtain billowed before the open windowsill. "Guess no homework tonight?" I taunted. "What a shame, I wanted to play the naughty teacher again. Figured that serenade hit your target, baby."

I traversed the laundry pile like a mountain goat, then

drummed my fingers against the other door. The hinges yawned as I pressed into her bedroom. "Perhaps you're ready and waiting in there? This is a sexy game of hide-and-seek." *All right, that sounded fun.*

Would Kinsley know where to hide or how to defend herself from men such as the one who peeked like a nightmare beneath her bed? *Come on. What was I working with, here—a total amateur?* Without a doubt, in the tritest of hidey-holes, I spied the unmistakable sheen of metal glinting in a telling gray against the light spilling into her room.

"Oh, naughty girl. You're keeping a secret. Perhaps I am not enough for you?"

Just as he took aim, the steel toe of my boot kicked the gun from his hand, and the cruel grain of the textured sole ground onto his fingers, ripping a cry of pain from his lips. Lucky for him, his face wasn't within reach. He had no choice but to expose himself.

I strolled into her en suite to give him a sporting chance and check that he was flying solo. My quarry rolled into the open with a clumsy dash for the hallway. Endorphins rushed like a feeding frenzy with the thrill of the chase!

"Not so fast, you sick—" Threats and names rained from my American imitation until I pinned his wrists behind his back by C-cups and straps. Wadded panties stuffed in his mouth muffled his pained screams. Each knuckle-bruising blow to areas of great reaction, with no exterior bloodshed, sent tingling pleasure spiraling like foreplay for the torment that lie ahead for him while I imagined the happy endings that lay in store to keep him from getting his hands on her. "Shall we take this back to my place?" I asked with suave sadism as I placed him into a chokehold and chopped his neck and shoulder with a brachial stun—pausing our cat-and-mouse play as he crumpled, passed out.

Hoisting his frame of no meager size over one shoulder, no sooner had I turned off the lights, did light of a different type shine into the windows and curve onto the walls before vanishing. *Someone was home!*

Shit!

The man's limp body jostled with my hustle into the study to pry that window wide open. He *had* come in this way because there was no screen to keep me from dropping him from the second story to the sprinkler damp soil below. Had I not written him onto the list myself, I may have felt sorry for the shoddy landing with nothing to help break his fall. Who knows? Perhaps the impact had done the rest of my job for me?

Now to get the hell out of here and inspect the bastard!

At the sound of her humming and the thrum of every step up the stairs, Kinsley had arrived, and our fates were in peril if I didn't find a place to hide this instant!

CHAPTER 26
KINSLEY

The driveway was empty.

"Thank God no one's home." I'd be able to slink back into my apartment without Daddy spying my naughty appearance. A late weeknight never stopped my parents from having fun with their friends. When my mom's SUV slept inside the garage, that meant that they'd gone out for drinks. If she took her vehicle, she left the garage door cracked at the bottom. No cracks tonight. Daddy was designated driver. Mom would be a handful.

So glad Daddy couldn't pester me about my evening at work with Jase.

Across the street, the slutty teen-aged dream from a few doors down was sucking face with a guy at the top of the slide. His hand was up her shirt. Her father would shoot him if he realized she wasn't the angel asleep in her room on a school night. "Hey, guys, you mind keeping it clean for the littles that play there in the morning?" I called, never having much tolerance for watching someone trash their self-esteem.

"Aren't *you* one to talk, daddy's girl," she sneered.

Huh?

The guy took off with the promise to call her. She gave a prissy pout and flipped me off while I shrugged her attitude off and mounted the stairs. *What was her damage? She should be thanking me for doing her a favor.*

When I walked inside, I swiped at my eye makeup and smacked the light switch with frustration at my sloppy mistake. I turned to snap the deadbolt. *Wait! I hadn't used my keys to get in!*

"What the hell?" I whispered and held my breath. Nothing moved. The only sound came from the ticking clock. I rushed to the refrigerator, then sighed with a hand to my chest.

No creamer. Mom must've stolen my coffee creamer again and forgotten to lock up after herself. "Thank you, Jesus, but good grief is Mom a hypocrite."

Irritated and relieved, I spilled every heavy cent and business card from my apron onto the coffee table, then heaved the tight shirt over my head. I shifted my shoulders as I adjusted the girls inside this crazy bra, half-tempted to pull the heavy curtains and unburden myself of this under-wire and lace. All I wanted was a shower and sleep.

"Son of a bitch!" I toppled over my own feet and caught myself against the floor as I tried to peel my legs from these damn shorts. In a bit of a fit, my tennis shoes flew from my feet against the baseboards in the hallway while I vented about Marcus's uniforms the way I wanted to. "Let's dress Marcus in nothing more than Spanx and see how his frank and beans feel after being smashed and outlined for hours with women copping feels! What am I saying? He'd love that. Ugh! I hate reeking like a beer-drenched wench!"

I peppered the laundry pile with the stinky uniform, then sank down before the mirror at the end of the hallway like my reflection was my only friend. "You look tired." My fingers reached out to touch the glass where wisps of hair rested against my forehead.

"Isn't life just so charmed because you make bank on tips? And all those medals! My, how many do you have now? Like a hundred? Oh, a hundred and two? My mistake. You're lucky. You don't even have to try. Scholarship, good looks, outrunning everyone in everything, aren't you babes? And isn't it just heaven how Jase Taylor sang to you? I bet you're not even grateful and probably still won't sleep with him. Then again, it's common knowledge you're a snobby prude who thinks you're better than everyone else around you. Poor thing. Alienated on that island of achievement with no one to keep you company."

I touched my face and pushed the wisps away like my mother would, tried seeing myself from her eyes. She'd been so afraid of that necklace. I grinned at my reflection.

"But wait!" I said to myself. "There's more! Hold, please."

I sought the velveteen box and opened up to show my reflection the necklace inside. She gasped and asked, "Is this real? Who gave you such pretty jewelry?" I tossed my head on an uppity laugh and waved my hand like this were nothing. "Why, I haven't a clue, love," I told her in a British accent. "But perhaps they came from the expensive man in the expensive suit with the best cologne in the world. Who's that you ask?" I scoffed at her and removed the necklace, secured the clasp at the nape of my neck, then admired the way her chin lifted and how her heavily made-up eyes sparkled with the emeralds and diamonds. "He's dangerous," I said, my chin and voice dropping. "Like this necklace. And the way you stare at me from stranger's eyes. Where's your innocence? You are scary."

I ran my fingers over the jewels, the flesh plumped by this bra, trailed my hand down the line between my abdominal muscles, stopped at my navel.

"Who are you, and what do you really want?"

How many times I'd asked myself that question at crossroads, but never in this capacity. As a grown woman. No more *where do I want 'this' to take me in adulthood?* I need a solution.

Does Jase have a place in the new phase, or will his recipe for a relationship call for sacrificing dreams? Do we even match?

My previous internship ended three months ago. Now I'd received letters of acknowledgment and consideration from the ones I'd applied to. Suspense was a nasty thing. I could always become Daddy's assistant. That also kept me here for Mr. Taylor if the internship downtown wasn't mine. The other one was upstate.

Was Jase ready or capable of hanging up that notched belt for a long-distance relationship neither of us knew would work?

Mom would have smacked my bottom at the direction my thoughts headed.

"You talk and think too much," I muttered to my reflection. Rather than remove the necklace, I wore this persona while I closed the heavy drapes in the living room, then scooped the tips in my hands and hauled the money to the lock box in my closet. The change went into a five-gallon jug. On the way to my room, the twenty-dollar-bill with the writing fluttered to the floor. I squatted to read the handwriting: *"Kinsley, you're a fire starter. Call me. Pat."*

"Ugh! Do guys think this works? I can't believe he had the nerve to say that to me before he left. Hmm...Jase pro: he's big and mean enough to scare jerks like this. Then again, that could also be a con for my guy friends. He might scare them all away. Which doesn't make sense because this guy, Pat, had been in front of Jase and had no problem giving me this with him watching."

I rolled my eyes and scaled the mountain of laundry. *Only—?*

Fragrance sucked through my nose like I should have had lines chopped on a table and that twenty as a straw. I'd never done drugs, never would, but I wasn't an idiot.

"Oh, God, please tell me he brushed off on me somewhere! How had I not smelled him before?"

I rushed into my bedroom and dumped the change on the foot of my bed, then hastened out to the laundry pile. On my knees, I flung dirty clothes, not caring where the stray twenty landed in the mayhem. "Where's my shirt? It must be around here! For goodness sakes! I smell him now!"

In the elevator and stairwell, the pirate had *the* most wonderful cologne I'd ever gotten my nose close to. His scent was a stain on the pirate coat I'd never wanted removed but faded after some months. Since then, I'd been on a secret quest to pin his fragrance down in stores without luck.

At my father's building, I'd smelled him twice since. The first time I hadn't given credence because he hadn't studied me with an ounce of recollection. Days ago, I'd complimented him, and he'd brushed my hand with his fingers. We had an undeniable chemistry, and he knew who I was and wasn't running away. Instead, he played games like a guerrilla fighter. Dart in, dart back out, repeat. To what end?

In my madness, I cursed about Jase, about the pirate, about men such as Rustin, and who I expected Jase to still be. Every stale liquor-stained uniform made me cringe. After five minutes, I realized there was no single article of clothing. Tears collected in my eyes as I stared down my reflection in the mirror again. That dangerous queen reduced to a desperate princess, she appeared confused.

"Longing for something you can't have? Shouldn't have,

and won't have if you respect the man who poured his heart out tonight?"

But here, I didn't have to pretend to be a better person. That reflection could be whoever she wanted to be, and deep down, the give a damn was getting harder to care about along with every 'should'.

When the phone rang, I ran to answer as if the person on the other end would pull me from this defiance and place me back into the skin of the good girl I'd always been. The one who'd choose a longtime crush over a mysterious stranger and never keep expensive gifts she could never wear in the light of day.

CHAPTER 27

KLIVE

Time's up! Kinsley's coming!

As I grappled for a place to hide, I understood why the rogue fireman picked such a childish space to conceal himself; there was nowhere to hide! I settled for the window and was about to take the branch when a teen shouted down the street as she looked back this way with her finger in the air.

Bollocks! Because things weren't perilous enough!

The closing windowpane slammed too loud. *Shit! I was damn near tempted to reveal myself and deal with her!* She was closing in on a situation that neither of us wished for. *Marcus was supposed to keep her at work, dammit!*

Instead of being as cocked-up as the Inferno novice, I leapt into the laundry area, whittled into the small space between the wall and the washing machine, at war with the clothes pile as I wrestled the accordion doors closed. Several articles of clothing hung from hangers on a bar over the washer and dryer, and I silently slid them close to further conceal myself. My fingers touched crushed velvet, and I knew. *My pirate coat!* I pat the inside pocket for the Bowie knife but found the pouch empty.

Through the slats, the living room became visible when she hit the lights. A terrifying thrill came with being able to see her without her seeing me. Like a two-way mirror, so long as she kept the bloody doors closed. More trepidation, not of the thrilling variety, accompanied the ways this might end. *What would I do if she caught me?*

Bile burned my esophagus when Kinsley turned to examine the door she'd slammed shut and placed a hand to her chest. *Had she not left the door unlocked?*

As she disappeared into the kitchen, visions played of these doors pulling apart. My hand smothering her scream of horror while she tumbled back against the wall or into the bathroom, every soft emotion vanishing with the instinct to survive. *Would she run? Fight? Faint? Would I knock her out, try to reason with her, mistakenly kill her in the mayhem?*

The idea made me shudder, but which would win out? *The Caveman or Casanova?* Ha! Both if I knocked her over the head and trapped her in my lair. Coming home from work would be far more invigorating! Nice thought, but the more consumed I became in this infatuation, the more rid of the passion I longed to be.

Thinking straight within her realm was impossible, and her presence played cricket with my conscience, swatted my contrasting emotions back and forth between wickets!

No! This wasn't happening! Please, God....

She crossed into the living area and ripped the top over her head.

My mouth became as dry as the Sahara. I didn't want to be this peeping pervert, but how could I resist? My eyes squeezed shut, but the gentleman gave up while the male gave in and relished the bottom half of the uniform peeling past her hips, down her muscular thighs, revealing cotton panties. The full curves of her breasts threatened to spill from her bra as she bent over and manipulated the stubborn material.

My fantasy paused, her hum replaced by frustrated grunts and curses. I stifled a laugh! Not at what she said. That part was hard to make out—except for Marcus's name—as she toppled over her own feet. She caught herself and wrestled the shorts off in a tizzy, kicking her legs as one swats at a bee invisible to everyone else, her shoes flying into the wall close by. Perhaps I should tell Marcus how pleased his star server was with her new uniforms. I cupped my laugh at her bitching about his 'frank and beans' being outlined and felt up.

The haze of lust dimmed as she spoke to herself, revealing a very raw and intimate peek into that mind. I stared through the slats, riveted on every word, until she vanished and reappeared with a square jewelry box she presented to her reflection. My breathing seized when she removed the most exquisite necklace encrusted with diamonds and emeralds she thought came from the expensive man in the expensive suit. *Me?* She had mentioned my cologne, unless there was another who wore cologne she loved. *Who the hell else could he be and who was he that he bought that anchor for her neck?!*

The purpose of this visit clicked back in place with a new type of anger so alien, so...so...hell, *what is this?*

Ponder later! Get out! Kill the dunce eating the daisies in Kinsley's flowerbed, then figure out where the hell this necklace came from!

She set the box on the floor. I nearly sagged against my coat when she ran her hand over the jewels then her body, down, down. She stopped shy of those panties and gave a magnificent view when she charged into the living room to scoop change into her palms. This bra was good, but she'd be lethal in lingerie, especially with that necklace. Some emerald earrings set in black gold to mimic her eyes. *Shit!*

She paused in the hallway when the money the Inferno asshole had handed her drifted to the clothing pile. His handwriting chunky and legible in black marker. She groaned after reading his words. I agreed with her irritation. If this were the sort of flirtation she received on a regular basis, shouldn't be too hard to knock her out of her knickers with a respectable effort. Shag her with that necklace on to spite the buyer!

My breath caught as she rose, but stopped midstride, inches from where I stood. Her head angled to inhale the oxygen deprived of me, and a foolish mistake as green as the irises peering my way glared me in the face: *wear nothing scented when entering another's domain!*

I wanted to throw a childish fit as she'd done, but holding still remained my only option. *Kinsley...back off, love...don't open the doors!* I prayed hard while she sniffed to find the source.

"Oh, God, please tell me he brushed off on me somewhere!" She ran into her room. I breathed for the split-second she took to drop the change, then drop to the floor near my feet! *Oh, to have her this way under different circumstances!*

"Where's my shirt?" Kinsley begged. "It must be around here! For goodness sakes! I smell him now! Why, God, what are you doing? My pirate! I know he's the guy from the beach! The elevator! I know they're the same man, and he's so freaking fine in every capacity, and we match and that's bad because I know he's not as nice as he looks, and he's as dangerous as the necklace he placed around my neck! Maybe he knows I'm not as nice as I look, either. You know I don't mean to be a bad girl and have bad thoughts. That's what this has to be, right? Some rebellious crisis before graduation like the cold feet a bride gets or something, but come on! Jase Taylor is the last person I should ever end up with!"

She vented in a fury, ripping dirty clothes up to her nose,

gagging at what she found. I breathed as shallow as possible, relieved, yet disturbed that she did think I was the buyer. All of this didn't stop me from being interested in what swam inside that wondering mind of hers. These insights gave me an unfair advantage over Jase Taylor, but I never professed to playing fair. Ironic she thought Jase to be the last person she should end up with when I was, but she knew better. Like fruit in the garden, a woman always desires most what she's denied.

She slumped in defeat, inhaling, sighing to the heavens and pleading forgiveness from her Lord for her thoughts. I smiled, flattered with how she loved my scent and longed for more of the knots I'd tied her into. I wondered if she might be as angry as I imagined were she to discover me. *Ha! Probably worse, considering our first encounter.*

"What is it about wanting what you shouldn't have?" she asked God. "That is why Jase wants me, why Rustin has a stupid crush, right? It's weird. Lord, how do I do this? And what about this man? Like you combined my favorite posters into one person." Her head tilted on a groan. *Score!* "Show me what to do. Who to pick beyond my foolish bias?" She huffed, then reached up for the handle on the accordion door in a horrific twist of irony!

CHAPTER 28
KLIVE

Music filled the silence. Kinsley bolted as her phone rang.

Hallelujah!

Every tense muscle sagged against the wall at my back, a silent praise going up to the textured ceiling.

"Constance!" Kinsley cheered and placed the phone on speaker.

"Kinsley effing Hayes!" her friend's voice sounded through the apartment. "I came to see you after my gig by the beach finished, but you're not at work. Where you at?"

"Aw, I'm sorry. Marcus keeps sending me home early from the crap that happened with Sara. He hasn't told me much, but I'm not stupid."

"Give me a break," Constance snorted. "What bartender hasn't endured harassment by a biker or five? Goes with the territory. Sara can't complain when she flirts with anyone who carries a wallet."

"Ugh. You sound like the day crowd down-lookers. They talk open trash about the bar, our new uniforms, they're terrible tippers. If they don't like the place, why not go somewhere else? There is no way Sara pays her bills with the early shift." Kinsley broke off. "Are you smoking?"

"Yes, just one, and I don't want to hear about how much prettier I'd be if I wasn't. We all have vices. Let's skip to the cool stuff. Everyone's gossiping about how the headliner serenaded you tonight! He's almost done, but I can tell Jase's deflated without you here."

The first of several squeals followed that statement.

Shoot me now.

Constance exhaled what I guessed to be smoke against her phone. "The whole bar is talking about it. But as your purity partner, I need every detail to gauge your level of risk. Sounds high if these sluts are any sign. They're ticked." *Purity partner?*

Kinsley sighed. "Oh, Constance, I wish you'd been there. Why weren't you? Your name was on the schedule."

"Stick to your story, then I'll explain."

"Jase was so romantic ..." Kinsley gushed and rushed through the events the way a child reads a Christmas list to Santa.

Meanwhile, in my mind, every recounted song translated to a sexual position Taylor planned once Kinsley dropped her panties.

Slaying my disappointment proved difficult considering how hard a time she had given *me*, a stranger, on the lift. But here she was, able to shift from sad to giddy in a flash. The way she'd plastered her smile at work then come home torn up said everything. This young woman concealed her true feelings, but why?

"How do you feel about it?" her friend asked once Kinsley came up for air.

"Happy. Who wouldn't be?"

I rolled my eyes, desperate to shake the truth from her.

"Agreed," her friend said, "but I'm weirded out by it." My

interest piqued, and Kinsley queried in kind. "Jase was the one who taught *me* you never, pardon my French, shit where you eat, or piss where you drink. He's going against his own rule by pursuing you."

That's because Taylor has a bigger male pissing all over his territory.

"Makes no sense. Don't hate me for this, Kins, but it's no secret you're a prude, and I don't care if he says he's had this thing for you since you were teenagers. What's he going to do when you won't give it up after a few dates, or at all? *You'd* better hold out after all the years of sacrifice."

"Constance, I've been wracking my brain about this for the past month!" Kinsley's cheeks flushed pink with the same sadness I'd seen on her in the laundry pile. As she stood before me once more, I expected her to collapse into the mess like she'd slumped when she'd arrived home.

"Past *month*?" Constance gasped. "There's more and you haven't told me? Kins, this is more dangerous than a single serenade."

What followed was a fair and informative debate on my prospective protégé's conduct and revealing on Kinsley's not-so-strong suits.

"Maybe I'm wrong, and it's possible a man can change." *Give me a bloody break!* "Kins, your choices are your own, but if you get with Jase, you need to get dirty and clean up."

"Come again?" she asked.

"Jase is a dirty man, but he is a neat freak, OCD style."

"I thought you said you never—how would you know?" Kinsley breathed, dread straining her voice.

"Ease up, I haven't, but I still broke his rule by accident. And ours...."

"Constance...what are you talking about? Is it why you weren't performing with him?"

"Yes, Kins! I am working my ass off to behave, but I'm a twenty-eight-year-old woman with needs, desires, living in the twenty-first century of free love!" Constance had vanished and given way to a whiny girl. "I'm not sure I even want a husband one day, and what if you don't either? Have you ever thought of what will happen if you fall in love with your career and decide you don't want to get married? Are you staying celibate forever? Can't I sacrifice smokes instead of sex and still be your purity partner? I can't keep doing this! Once you start, it's so hard to stop!"

Kinsley growled at Constance's meltdown while I wanted to do the same. *Some of us had people to kill and a nap to take before the office in the morning.*

"Get a grip, Constance. Tell me what happened and how it pertains to Jase!"

Kinsley bordered on tears like Taylor had already broken her heart. Her chest heaved. Oh, to yank her into my arms and order her not to love what was bad.

I was bad, dammit, but what did it matter if she would fall into a set of bad arms either way?

Constance cleared her throat. "I didn't sleep with Jase, and I never will, though you should check and see if Sara has. I bet her customers are getting jealous of one another. Maybe that's why the bikers are suddenly interested in finding her."

"Constance! What the *hell* has gotten into you? I know you two don't get along, but damn. I don't trash your friends that I hate. Quit deflecting! You slept with someone, and I'm irritated, but it's always meant more to me than it does to you."

They both huffed and sat for thoughtful seconds.

"Okay. I deserved that. Look, I slept with Rustin. Jase wasn't pleased when I came downstairs to make breakfast and didn't wash my dishes. Not to mention how pissed he was that I was even at his house.

I mean, like we haven't been friends forever?"

"*Rustin?*" Kinsley interrupted in shock.

"Yes, Kins. The sexy blond with boots made for walking all over you in the bedroom. If I'd known he was staying, let alone planning on joining Rock-N-Awe, I wouldn't have given him more than a smile. It was a desperate moment, and tequila makes you do things those whiny country songs aren't lying about. Now I'm so nervous, I've been avoiding Jase, and I think I might have burned a valuable bridge, or at least set it on fire. He's mad at me, and he's a huge source of networking my gigs. If I don't make amends, my gigs might dry up."

Kinsley rolled her eyes. "First of all, you give him way too much credit. You have a gift. Sure, he's introduced you to great contacts, but your voice is what books your jobs. Second, he's *disappointed*. Two of his good friends making a bad judgment call. Who can blame him? He'll be in the middle if this goes sour. Third, you've been holding this crap in for like a month, so we're even. Sorry I made you feel you couldn't confess."

"It's not only disappointment. I'm telling you, he has Obsessive Compulsive Disorder bad, which means you need to quit calling out this tiny splinter in my eye and clean up that plank of an apartment in yours. And thank you, but, for real, you will be a huge disappointment to me if you go to bed with him after all your effort."

"I'm not going to bed with him. And my apartment isn't dirty." Kinsley merged the land mines into one major obstacle. "You can ask my mom because she was here. Stole my coffee creamer. Having zero rent is nice, but I have no privacy. So, you see, even if I was going to screw up and sleep with Jase, it's impossible because the parentals see and know everything. She even left my door unlocked when they're always on me about that."

Constance laughed and blew another breath against the

phone. "Your apartment is dirty, and I'm surprised your mom didn't do laundry and take the creamer as payment. And you can complain about zero rent and no privacy, but seriously, your dad still makes you breakfast. Your mom hides meals in your refrigerator and does your laundry. If you hate it, you can come split rent and utilities with me."

"Psh, whatever. She didn't do my laundry because I planned on washing clothes when I got home. Your call interrupted my chores."

"I can come over and help."

"That's sweet, but I am cleaning then going to bed. I may sleep in tomorrow."

"Wow, you *never* sleep in. I hurt you. Forgive me for letting you down," Constance told her.

"Forgive me if I end up letting you down."

"Kinsley Fallon Hayes. What do you always tell me? If you leave room for failure, you'll fail. But you always have my forgiveness."

Kinsley sighed and sauntered into the hallway holding the phone in her palm and checking for an eyelash in the mirror. "I just feel like everyone is alive in motion around me while I'm sitting still. Not trying to fail, just have less and less in common with the people around me. I'm lonely. That's stupid isn't it?"

"No. Not stupid. But you're tired and have a lot on your mind. I doubt you're sleeping enough. How much have you had to eat and drink?"

Kinsley covered her stomach and cringed. "I just ate, and I've got a bottle of water I'm nursing."

"Right...you never eat or drink enough. You're gonna put yourself in the hospital. Maybe you should sleep in and report back tomorrow. You may not feel lonely or envious of your peers with a clear mind," Constance reasoned. "Go. Hang up. Eat. Drink. Sleep. We'll talk. Bye, babes."

"Bye, Constance." Kinsley tapped her phone and leaned her forehead against the mirror.

I couldn't help wishing to steal these petty worries from her mind and make her something to eat. At the same time, I both envied and related with her, unable to relate to my peers for the restrictions on my lifestyle and continuously staying on the move to the point of burn-out and hunger.

She turned, and the door in front of the washing machine yanked open. Every scenario of what came next swam like lottery balls.

Whose number would tumble forth? Hers or my own?

DEAR READER,

Thank you for reading this installment of my series. If you enjoyed this wild ride, will you please take a moment to leave me a review?

Anytime a new review is left, the algorithms recommend my work to another reader like you.

Unsure of what to say? Don't worry, so are a lot of readers, but even one-liners as simple as "I loved it" or "Pick it up, you won't be sorry" can make a huge difference for an independent author like myself.

When you're done, please follow me and sign up at my website for the Lit with Lynnie newsletter to stay in touch.

Thank you from the bottom of my heart.

X - Lynessa

www.lynessalayne.com
www.tropiconbookexpo.com

ACKNOWLEDGMENTS

To Christ Yeshua. I wouldn't be here if you hadn't seen me next to death in the darkness, taken me by the hand and said, "Talitha cumi: little girl, arise." —Mark 5:41. You are the breath in my body, apart from which I can do nothing, but with you I can do anything. I am forever grateful for your boundless love, mercy, forgiveness, and above all, your laying your life down so we may be forgiven of our sins and welcomed into your kingdom. Thank you for leaving the 99 to chase me down, for setting a place for me at your table, for saving a wretch like me.

To Ashley, my cover designer and editor, but above all my author bestie. How many years did this take? You helped me come from concept to reality. Thank you for bearing with my flip-flopping and insecurity, all the doubts. Your own courage feeds mine and I'm grateful for every step that you took to help me get here. I couldn't have done this series glow-up without you.

To AJ, my associate editor, consultant, and beloved battle buddy. AJ has a Bachelors in Communication-Journalism. He served five combat tours in Iraq and Afghanistan and over twenty-four years in the United States armed forces. Thank you for your leadership, friendship and willingness to allow me ugly moments of frustration. I'm grateful you never gave up, never surrendered and taught me to follow suit when I wanted to throw this manuscript in the trash and never look back.

To my children. You better not be reading this until you're adults, but each of you pushed me to never give up. You've pressed me forward knowing I wasn't writing for children's eyes. You loved me for me, the sloppy, clumsy, imperfect woman who felt she never measured up to other mothers, but in your hearts surpassed them all as I unknowingly brought you peace with the sounds of my fingers on the keyboard; music in the background, chores completed while having living room dance parties, family meetings around the dinner table. You allow normalcy to bless you. In turn, you bless me far beyond this and anything I write. This series was a personal goal, but YOU are the dream and my most valued treasure. My quiver is full.

ABOUT THE AUTHOR

Lynessa is an award winning author and professional book formatter. Though she builds worlds like a fantasy author, she prefers settings you can visit with characters you could know.

She has a passion for high strangeness, true crime, fringe, unraveling mysteries, and solving puzzles. Life has taught her to never take anyone or anything at face value. She enjoys research and investigation along with delving into deep topics with her retired crime-fighting hubby.

She is a military wife and homeschools her children deep in the heart of Texas where she was born and raised.

When she's not writing, she is best known for hosting and organizing TropiCon Book Expo & Writing Convention.